H. G. Wells

隱形人

The Invisible Man

改寫 _ Donatella Velluti

譯者 _ 劉嘉珮

About Your Book

🎧 Listen to the story.

🗩 Talk about the story.

⭐ⓟ Prepare for Cambridge English Exams: B1 Preliminary.

[FACT FILE] Read informative fact files which develop themes from the story.

[LIFE SKILL] Draw comparisons between the story and contemporary life.

e-ZONE ONLINE ACTIVITIES Go to Helbling e-zone to do activities.

For the Teacher

A state-of-the-art interactive learning environment with 1000s of free online self-correcting activities for your chosen readers.

Go to our Readers Resource site for information on using readers and downloadable Resource Sheets, photocopiable Worksheets and Answer Keys. Plus free sample tracks from the story.
helbling.com/english

For lots of great ideas on using Graded Readers, consult Reading Matters, the Teacher's Guide to using Helbling Readers.

Contents

Herbert George Wells (or H. G. Wells) is considered, along with the French writer Jules Verne, to be the father of science fiction[1]. He was born in Bromley, near London, in 1880, to a modest family. When he was eight, he broke his leg and was confined[2] to bed for a long time. His father brought him books from the local library and he became a keen[3] reader.

Due to his family's economic situation, Wells could not go to school, but he read and studied on his own. He became so proficient[4] that a school offered him the position of student-teacher. This meant that he was able to pay for his own education by teaching younger pupils.

He then went to Imperial College in London to study biology, and graduated in zoology at the University of London.

His novels have been hugely popular since their publication, and some of them have become films. He invented themes that became classic in science fiction. He also predicted technological developments that became reality, like space travel. A crater [5] on the dark side of the Moon is named after him. Some of his stories are very realistic: Orson Welles' radio adaptation [6] of his novel *The War of the Worlds* convinced people that an invasion [7] from Mars was really happening in New Jersey. He also wrote about social justice and human rights.

H. G. Wells died in London in 1946, probably from a heart attack [8].

1 science fiction 科幻小說
2 confined [kən`faɪnd] (a.) 把……局限在
3 keen [kin] (a.) 熱衷的
4 proficient [prə`fɪʃənt] (a.) 熟練的；精通的
5 crater [`kretɚ] (n.) 坑
6 adaptation [ˌædəp`teʃən] (n.) 改編
7 invasion [ɪn`veʒən] (n.) 入侵
8 heart attack 心肌梗塞

Today many people enjoy stories about time travel, invasions by strange beings from other planets, etc. But in 1895, when H. G. Wells published his first novel, *The Time Machine*, about a journey to the future, readers knew only two genres[1] in fiction. One was realism[2], i.e. fiction about the real world (past or present), and the second was fantasy[3], i.e. fiction about impossible worlds, creatures and events. H. G. Wells (and Jules Verne), like the scientists in their stories, *invented* a new genre: science fiction. Science fiction is based on future developments in science and technology. *The Time Machine* was an instant success.

The late nineteenth century was a time of technological discoveries. These discoveries were suddenly changing society and the way people lived, and the changes were happening very quickly. New questions needed answers: what will be the effect [4] of technology on society? Are scientists going too far? And above all: if something is technologically possible, should we automatically create it? Is there a danger that evil people will gain control of the new technology and use it to their advantage [5]? In science fiction, writers and readers are able to explore [6] their feelings about whether scientific advances [7] are always good for people and the planet [8].

The Invisible Man, published in 1897, was H. G. Well's second science fiction novel. It starts with the arrival of a mysterious stranger in a small village in southern England during a snow storm, and explores some difficult questions about scientific inventions.

---

1 genre [ˈʒɑnrə] (n.)〔法〕文藝作品之類型
2 realism [ˈrɪəl͵ɪzəm] (n.) 寫實主義
3 fantasy [ˈfæntəsɪ] (n.) 奇幻作品
4 effect [ɪˈfɛkt] (n.) 影響
5 advantage [ədˈvæntɪdʒ] (n.) 利益；優點
6 explore [ɪkˈsplor] (v.) 探索
7 advance [ədˈvæns] (n.) 發展；進步
8 planet [ˈplænɪt] (n.) 行星

From Horror to Science Fiction

MARY SHELLEY'S

FRANKENSTEIN

What happens when science goes beyond nature? This is one of the main themes of *The Invisible Man*. However, it was not the first time that this theme appeared in literature. It is also at the heart of Mary Shelley's *Frankenstein*, first published in 1818.

Mary Shelley
(1797–1851)

In this novel, Victor Frankenstein, a brilliant young scientist builds a body using parts of corpses[1] and then brings it to life. However, the "Creature" (as he is called in the book) is a monster and Frankenstein rejects[2] him. The Creature runs away and discovers that his appearance terrifies people. In his anger against his "father," he kills Victor's youngest brother.

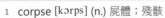

"FRANKENSTEIN"
THE MAN WHO MADE A MONSTER

CARL LAEMMLE
presents

A UNIVERSAL
PICTURE

He is very lonely and begs Victor for a female companion. When Victor refuses, the Creature kills Victor's wife and also his best friend. In the end the experiment[3] destroys[4] both the creator and the creation.

1 corpse [kɔrps] (n.) 屍體；殘骸
2 reject [rɪˋdʒɛkt] (v.) 拒絕
3 experiment [ɪkˋspɛrəmənt] (n.) 實驗
4 destroy [dɪˋstrɔɪ] (v.) 毀滅

9

Frankenstein raises important questions about the relationship between science and ethics[1]. This is why the most famous horror story of all time is also a precursor[2] of science fiction.

The tragedy occurs because Victor is unable to deal with the terrible results of his experiment. He does the experiment because he is obsessed[3], without thinking of the possible consequences[4]. Victor tries to protect the people he loves, but fails. He knows he was the real cause of their deaths and feels huge guilt.

It is Victor's inability to manage the results of his experiment that makes the Creature a real monster. At first the Creature hides in the woods and secretly helps a poor family that lives nearby. He tries to be part of society: he learns to speak by listening to the family, then he finds some books and teaches himself to read and write. But when he tries to connect with the family, they reject him in fear, and he becomes desperate[5].

He understands that without Victor's help, he will always be an outcast[6]. He asks for a companion, but Victor will not create one because he believes the Creature is bad. He fears that if he gives the Creature a wife, they will bring an evil race into the world. Victor's refusal means that the Creature must live a life of total isolation[7], so he decides to make Victor's life desperate and lonely, too. The story is a true tragedy.

- What happens when human intelligence produces a monster?
- And who is really the monster?
- What happens when a human makes a scientific discovery and uses it in a monstrous way? These are some of the questions *Frankenstein* and *The Invisible Man* raised. The world is still discussing them today.

1 ethics [ˈɛθɪks] (n.) 倫理道德
2 precursor [priˈkɜsɚ] (n.) 先驅；前輩
3 obsessed [əbˈsɛst] (a.) 著迷的
4 consequence [ˈkɑnsəˌkwɛns] (n.) 後果
5 desperate [ˈdɛspərɪt] (a.) 絕望的
6 outcast [ˈaʊtˌkæst] (n.) 被逐出的人
7 isolation [ˌaɪslˈeʃən] (n.) 孤立

WHAT ARE YOU LOOKING AT?

SURVEILLANCE[1] SOCIETY

An old legend[2] tells the story of a man who knew what other people were thinking. He could read other people's minds and was unhappy as a result. He was lonely because nobody knew him the way he knew everybody else. One day he met another man who could read other people's minds. They instantly hated each other.

This is a reflection on the idea that we all want someone who understands us completely, but we also need privacy[3]. We need to be free to choose who has information about us and what they know about us. We need people to trust us even if they don't know everything about us. We feel uncomfortable when we know people are watching us. We need some "invisibility[4]." These are some of the reasons why privacy is a basic human right.

Article 12 of the Universal Declaration[5] of Human Rights says that everyone has the right to the protection of the law against interference[6] with their privacy or attacks on their privacy. This includes their family, home, correspondence[7] and also their reputation[8].

1 surveillance [sə`veləns] (n.) 監視
2 legend [`lɛdʒənd] (n.) 傳說;傳奇故事
3 privacy [`praɪvəsɪ] (n.) 隱私
4 invisibility [ˌɪnvɪzə`bɪlətɪ] (n.) 看不見
5 declaration [ˌdɛklə`reʃən] (n.) 宣言
6 interference [ˌɪntə`fɪrəns] (n.) 干預
7 correspondence [ˌkɔrə`spɑndəns]
   (n.) 通信(聯繫);(總稱)信件
8 reputation [ˌrɛpjə`teʃən] (n.) 聲譽

SO HOW MUCH PRIVACY DO YOU HAVE TODAY?

CCTV [1]

Every time you go into a shop, public building and many private buildings, and when you move through the streets of your town or city, you are filmed by CCTV cameras.

SOCIAL MEDIA

If you have a social media [2] account, you probably use it to share a lot of private information about yourself: your photos, where you are, what you are thinking, who you are with, what you are doing, other people's posts, who you follow and everything you "like" or react to.

Your personal data and all these activities are recorded and sold to data analysts. They produce a secret profile that describes you. How did you set your privacy settings? Can people you don't know see your page? Who can see your data? What do they do with your data? Who can see your secret profile? Do you know what that profile says about you?

YOUR MOBILE PHONE

You are probably terrified by the thought of losing your mobile phone, because so much of your "life" is in it. However, how private is all that life you store³ in your phone? Your location, every text message, every phone call, every app⁴ you use and every website you visit are logged⁵. Do you know what happens to these logs? Do you know who can access them?

- Which of these types of surveillance are acceptable to you? Why?
- Which of them are not? Why?

---

1 CCTV 監視器（closed-circuit television）
2 media [`midɪə] (n.) 媒體（medium 的複數）
3 store [stor] (v.) 儲存
4 app [æp] (n.) 應用程式（application 的縮寫）
5 log [lɔg] (v.) (n.) 登錄

CHARACTERS

Coach
and
Horses

Mr Hall

Mrs Hall

Dr Kemp

Colonel Adye

The Invisible Man

Mr Bunting

Mr Jaffers

Mr Thomas Marvel

Mr Teddy Henfrey

17

Before Reading

1 Match the jobs to the descriptions of what the characters do.

① policeman

② scientist

③ doctor

④ landlady

⑤ tramp

⑥ chief of police

⑦ vicar

_____ [a] Dr Kemp studies and researches science.

_____ [b] Mrs Hall is the owner of an inn.

_____ [c] Mr Bunting is a priest in the Church of England.

_____ [d] Mr Cuss looks after people who are ill.

_____ [e] Mr Jaffers is called when someone breaks the law.

_____ [f] Colonel Adye is in charge of all policemen in the village.

_____ [g] Mr Marvel has no home, job or money; he lives on charity.

2 Read the two character descriptions from the story. Which characters from Exercise **1** are they describing?

[a] _____ had a large face, a big nose, a wide mouth and a strange beard. He was fat, with short arms and legs. He wore a very old silk hat, and his coat had shoelaces instead of buttons. He was sitting by the roadside, not far from Iping.

b It was early evening and
_____, a tall and slender
young man, was sitting in his
study on the hill overlooking Port
Burdock, doing some important
scientific research.

3 Find the two place names in Exercise **2**.
Then find out which part of England they are in.
Are they both real places?

4 Look at the diagrams and read the sentences.
Then complete the sentences using the words in color.

A glass is
transparent
and refracts light.

A mirror
reflects light.

A banana absorbs
most light, but
reflects yellow light.

a If an object _____ light, the light goes into the
object but doesn't go through it.

b If an object _____ light, the light goes through
it but it changes angle as soon as it enters the object.

c If an object _____ light, the light hits the object
and bounces from it.

5 Look at the pictures. Match the two sentence halves below. Then write the names under the pictures.

_____ [a] We use test tubes   [1] and cover a window.
_____ [b] Goggles are glasses   [2] that protect the eyes.
_____ [c] Shutters look like little doors [3] to cut trees and wood.
_____ [d] Handcuffs are put   [4] to stir a fire.
_____ [e] A poker is used   [5] and carries things.
_____ [f] We use an axe   [6] on a person's wrists.
_____ [g] A cart is pulled by a horse [7] in scientific experiments.

6 Read the extracts from *The Invisible Man*.
Answer the questions.

It was great. I felt like a man who could see in a city of the blind. But soon I realized that there were problems. I could avoid people coming towards me, but not people behind me. And crowds were dangerous for me.

I began to see the problems. I had no shelter and no clothes. If I wore the clothes, I lost all my advantage.

_____ a Why were people behind the Invisible Man a problem?

_____ b Why were crowds dangerous for him?

_____ c Why did the Invisible Man lose his advantage if he wore clothes?

7 Work with a partner.
Can you think of other disadvantages of being invisible?
What advantages are there?

8 Read the text and match the words in bold to their definitions.

Negative feelings can be difficult to manage, and different people respond differently. When something unexpected happens, people are surprised. If the surprise is great, they may take in air quickly. In other words, they may **gasp**. If it is an unpleasant surprise, people can be **startled**, and they will react in different ways. For example, a child may **stamp** their feet on the ground to express frustration and **exasperation**. Adults who are normally calm may become anxious and **distressed**. Others can become impatient and **irritable**, get angry at small things and **lose their temper** easily. When people are angry, some express it in private by **punching** things like pillows, but others can become **aggressive**. If they lose control, they can start **raving** about the situation or **smashing** things. It is very important to learn to recognize negative feelings when they start, so you can deal with them in a healthy way.

_____ ⓐ breaking something noisily, usually glass

_____ ⓑ annoyance about something you can do nothing about

_____ ⓒ hitting with one's fist

_____ ⓓ surprised, especially by something negative

_____ ⓔ in an angry and violent way

_____ ⓕ take a short, quick breath through the mouth because of surprise or pain

_____ ⓖ lose control and become angry suddenly

_____ ⓗ put one's foot down on the ground hard and noisily

_____ ⓘ very upset and worried

_____ ⓙ speaking in an uncontrolled way because you are angry (or ill)

_____ ⓚ easily annoyed

9 What do you think will happen in the story? Do you think the novel will have a happy ending?

1. The Strange Man's Arrival

The stranger came to Iping on the 29th of February, through a cold wind and snow storm, walking from Bramblehurst railway station with a large suitcase[1]. He was wrapped up[2] from head to foot, with big blue goggles[3], a scarf and a hat that together hid every bit of his face except the tip of his nose. There was snow on his shoulders and chest. He staggered[4] into the Coach and Horses more dead than alive and dropped his suitcase.

"A fire," he cried, "Please! A room and a fire!"

He followed Mrs Hall, the landlady[5], into the guest sitting room. She lit the fire and went into the kitchen. She started cooking the bacon, then went back into the sitting room to lay the table. Although the fire was burning nicely, she was surprised to see that the stranger was still wrapped up.

"Can I take your hat and coat, sir?" she said, "and give them a good dry in the kitchen?"

"No," he said looking out of the window. "I prefer to keep them on."

"Very well, sir," she said. "In a bit the room will be warmer."

1 suitcase [`sut,kes] (n.) 手提箱
2 wrap up 包裹住
3 goggles [`gɑglz] (n.) 〔複〕護目鏡
4 stagger [`stægɚ] (v.) 搖搖晃晃
5 landlady [`lænd,ledɪ] (n.) (旅館) 女主人

He didn't answer. Mrs Hall laid the table quickly and left the room. When she returned, he was still standing there.

She put down the eggs and bacon noisily, and said loudly, "Your lunch is served, sir."

"Thank you," he said, and did not move.

When Mrs Hall went back, she knocked and entered without waiting for an answer. The stranger was sitting at the table and moved quickly to pick something up from the floor.

She noticed his coat and hat on a chair in front of the fire. She looked at them and said, "May I take them to dry now?"

"Leave the hat," said her visitor, in a muffled [1] voice.

She turned and for a moment she was too surprised to speak.

He was still wearing his gloves and he was holding a white cloth over the lower part of his face. That was the reason for his muffled voice, but it was not what startled [2] Mrs Hall. It was the fact that all of his head above his blue goggles, including his ears, was covered by a white bandage [3]. The only visible part of his face was his pink nose. He was still wearing his scarf, and strands [4] of thick black hair were coming out between the bandages.

She put the hat back on the chair. "I didn't know, sir . . ." she began.

"Thank you," he said.

---

1 muffled ['mʌf!d] (a.)
   （聲音）被隔的；聽不太清的
2 startle ['stɑrt!] (v.) 使嚇一跳

3 bandage ['bændɪdʒ]
   (n.) 繃帶
4 strand [strænd] (n.) 縷

"I'll have it dried, sir," she said, and took his coat and left.

"The poor man has had an accident [5] or an operation [6] that disfigured [7] him," thought Mrs Hall as she put his coat in front of the kitchen fire.

Mrs Hall

- Why does Mrs Hall think the stranger has had an accident?

When she cleared away the stranger's lunch, he said that his luggage was at Bramblehurst station.

"Can I have it sent here?" he asked.

Mrs Hall said a cart [8] could go there the next day.

"Not earlier?"

Mrs Hall saw the opportunity to find out the reason for her guest's appearance. "It's a steep [9] road, sir," she said. "A cart lost control there about a year ago. Two men died. Accidents, sir, happen in a moment, don't they?"

"They do."

5 accident [ˈæksədənt] (n.) 意外；事故
6 operation [ˌɑpəˈreʃən] (n.) 手術
7 disfigure [dısˈfıgjɚ] (v.) 損毀……的外形；使難看
8 cart [kɑrt] (n.) 四輪運貨車；手推車
9 steep [stip] (a.) 陡峭的

"But people take a long time to get well again, don't they? My sister's son, Tom, cut his arm at work, and he was bandaged for three months. My sister had to do his bandages, and then undo them. So if you don't mind, sir, could I ask . . ."

He interrupted her. "Will you get me some matches? My pipe is out."

His rudeness[1] upset Mrs Hall. She stared[2] at him for a moment, then she went for the matches.

"Thanks," he said, turning his back to her to look out of the window.

"He's very sensitive on the topic of accidents and bandages," thought Mrs Hall. But his rudeness irritated[3] her.

He remained in the sitting room for the rest of the day.

The Stranger

1. What is unusual about the stranger?
2. Why do you think the stranger is rude?
3. If someone is rude to you, what do you do or say? Tell a partner.

---

1 rudeness ['rudnəs] (n.) 粗魯
2 stare [stɛr] (v.) 盯；凝視
3 irritate ['ɪrə,tet] (v.) 使惱怒；使煩躁

At four o'clock, Mrs Hall was trying to find the courage to go in and offer her visitor some tea. The man who repaired clocks, Teddy Henfrey, came into the bar, so she asked him to check the old clock in the sitting room.

She knocked on the door. When she entered, she saw her visitor asleep in the armchair, with his bandaged head on one side. The only light in the room was from the fire, which lit his goggles but left his face in darkness. For a second, she thought that he had an enormous mouth that filled the lower half of his face. Then he woke up and put his gloved hand over his mouth.

She brought the lamp in and saw him more clearly. He was holding the white cloth to his face, so she couldn't see his mouth.

"Well," she thought, "it was probably just a shadow."

"Would you mind, sir, if this man looks at the clock?" she asked.

"Go ahead," he said.

Mr Henfrey came in, but when he saw the stranger, he stopped suddenly.

The stranger greeted him, and then spoke to Mrs Hall. "Have you made any arrangements about my luggage at Bramblehurst?" he asked.

"I have," said Mrs Hall. "The postman will bring it tomorrow morning."

"Thank you," said the stranger. "I was too cold and tired earlier to explain that I am a scientist. My luggage contains my equipment[1]. I like to be alone when I do my research[2], so please don't disturb me. I had an accident and my eyes sometimes hurt so much that I have to be in the dark for hours. When that happens, the smallest interruption is very upsetting. Is this clear?"

"Certainly, sir," said Mrs Hall, and left the room.

Mr Henfrey started to work very slowly, hoping to discover more about the stranger.

"The weather . . ." Mr Henfrey began.

"Why don't you finish and go?" said the stranger, clearly irritated. "It's not a complicated[3] job."

"Certainly, sir," Mr Henfrey finished and left, but he was very upset.

---

1 equipment [ɪˈkwɪpmənt] (n.) 設備
2 research [rɪˈsɜtʃ] (n.) 研究
3 complicated [ˈkɑmpləˌketɪd] (a.) 複雜的

In the village he met Mrs Hall's husband, and he told him all about the stranger.

"Looks like a disguise[1], doesn't it?" said Mr Henfrey. "He's taken your rooms and he hasn't given a name. And he's got a lot of luggage coming tomorrow. He says it's equipment, but who knows? It could be anything."

Research

1. What does the stranger say about his work and how he works?
2. Do you believe him? Share ideas with a partner.

---

1 disguise [dɪsˋgaɪz] (n.) 偽裝；掩飾
2 strike [straɪk] (v.) 打；擊
  （動詞三態：strike–struck–struck, stricken）
3 violently [ˋvaɪələntlɪ] (adv.) 猛烈地
4 slam [slæm] (v.) 猛地關上

3. The Thousand and One Bottles

The next day the postman brought the stranger's luggage on his cart. Mr Hall was outside the inn, waiting to bring the luggage in and playing with the postman's dog.

The stranger came out wrapped up as usual. As soon as the postman's dog saw him, it began to growl angrily. Before the postman could stop it, the dog bit the stranger and tore his glove and trouser leg. The stranger rushed back into the inn and went up to his bedroom.

"I'd better go and see if he's all right," said Mr Hall.

He went upstairs and since the stranger's door was open, he walked in.

The room was dark. All he saw was a handless arm, then he was struck[2] violently[3] in the chest and thrown out of the room. The door was slammed[4] in his face and locked.

He stood there in shock and then went outside.

After a moment the dog began growling again.

"Hurry!" shouted an angry voice in the doorway. There stood the stranger, fully covered, with a different pair of gloves and trousers.

"Were you hurt, sir?" said the postman. "I'm really sorry, the dog . . ."

"Not a bit," said the stranger. "Bring my boxes in."

As the boxes were carried into the sitting room, the stranger unpacked them quickly. They contained hundreds of test tubes[1] and bottles with powders and liquids of all colors, some labeled Poison. And as soon as the boxes were unpacked, he started to work.

When Mrs Hall took his dinner to him, he was so absorbed[2] in his work that he did not hear her until she put the food on the table. Then he half-turned his head and immediately turned it away again. But she saw he wasn't wearing his goggles, and his eye sockets[3] seemed strangely empty.

Empty

1. What is the title of this novel?
2. What does "invisible" mean?
3. What things make us think that the stranger may be invisible?
4. What would you feel and think if you were Mr and Mrs Hall?

He put on his goggles again, and then turned towards her. "Please don't come in without knocking," he said in the exasperated [4] tone that was now normal for him.

"I knocked, but you . . ."

"Perhaps you did. But in my research—my very urgent and necessary research—the slightest interruption . . . I must ask you . . ."

He was so strange and aggressive [5] that Mrs Hall felt scared. But she was also losing her patience [6] with him.

"Certainly, sir. You can lock the door, you know. Any time."

"Yes," said the stranger. He turned and sat down with his back to her.

All afternoon he worked with the door locked. Once Mrs Hall heard a bang [7] and the sound of bottles ringing together, and she went to listen outside his door.

"I can't go on," he was raving [8]. "It's too much! It may take me all my life! Fool! Fool!"

And then all was silent again.

1 tube [tjub] (n.) 管
2 absorbed [əb'sɔrbd] (a.) 專注的
3 socket ['sɑkɪt] (n.) 窩；槽；臼
4 exasperated [ɪg'zæspə,retɪd] (a.) 激怒的
5 aggressive [ə'grɛsɪv] (a.) 侵略性的
6 patience ['peʃəns] (n.) 耐心；耐性
7 bang [bæŋ] (n.) 砰砰聲 (v.) 猛擊；猛撞
8 rave [rev] (v.) 狂亂地說

4. The Burglary¹ at the Vicarage²

Not much happened until Whit Monday³. The stranger spent all his time working in the sitting room and had no communication with the world outside the village. Most of the time he was extremely irritable⁴, and once or twice things were broken with sudden violence. He often talked to himself. Mrs Hall listened carefully, but she never understood what she heard. The children called him names and everybody disliked him.

The burglary at the vicarage happened on Whit Monday. Mrs Bunting, the vicar's⁵ wife, woke up suddenly before dawn, with the strange feeling that somebody was in the house. She heard the sound of bare⁶ feet, and she woke her husband as quietly as possible. In the dark, Mr Bunting put on his glasses and went out on the landing⁷ to listen. He heard noises in his study downstairs, and then a violent sneeze⁸.

He picked up the most obvious weapon, a poker⁹, and went down the stairs as noiselessly as he could. Mrs Bunting followed him.

---

1 burglary [ˋbɝglərɪ] (n.) 夜盜；搶劫
2 vicarage [ˋvɪkərɪdʒ] (n.) 教區；牧師住宅
3 Whit Monday 聖靈降臨節星期一
4 irritable [ˋɪrətəbl̩] (a.) 易怒的；急躁的
5 vicar [ˋvɪkɚ] (n.) 教區牧師
6 bare [bɛr] (a.) 裸的

7 landing [ˋlændɪŋ] (n.)
　各段樓梯之間的踏足平台
8 sneeze [sniz] (n.) 噴嚏；
　打噴嚏
9 poker [ˋpokɚ] (n.) 火鉗

The house was dark and quiet. Then something broke and there was the sound of rustling[1] paper. They heard someone swearing[2], then a match was struck and the study was filled with yellow light.

Mr and Mrs Bunting were now in the hall. Through the open door they could see the desk with a drawer open and a candle burning on the desk. But they could not see the burglar.

They heard the sound of rustling paper again—it was the savings[3] the vicar kept in the drawer. Holding the poker firmly, Mr Bunting rushed[4] into the room, closely followed by Mrs Bunting.

"Hands up!" he cried, and then stopped amazed—the room was completely empty.

For half a minute, perhaps, Mr and Mrs Bunting stood with their mouths open, then they looked everywhere. They couldn't find anybody, but the money was gone.

There was a violent sneeze in the kitchen. As they rushed into the kitchen, they saw the back door open. Nobody went in or out, but the door closed with a slam.

The Burglary

1. Who is the burglar?
2. Have you or someone you know had a burglary?
3. What happened? Tell a partner.

5. The Furniture That Went Mad [5]

The same day, Mr and Mrs Hall got up very early. As he was going down the stairs, Mr Hall noticed that the stranger's door was open. Then when he got downstairs he saw that the front door was not locked. He remembered locking it the night before.

He went upstairs and knocked on the stranger's door, then pushed the door open and entered. The room was empty and their guest's clothes and bandages were scattered [6] on the bed. He called his wife, who was downstairs.

"He's not in his room," he said, "but his clothes are. What's he doing without his clothes? And the front door is unlocked."

They thought they heard the front door open and shut, and someone sneezed on the stairs. Mr Hall thought it was his wife downstairs. She thought it was her husband upstairs.

As Mrs Hall joined her husband in the stranger's bedroom, an extraordinary thing happened. The stranger's clothes gathered themselves together and jumped onto the floor. Then the hat flew straight at Mrs Hall's face. And the chair rose in the air with its four legs pointed at Mrs Hall and flew towards her.

---

1   rustle [`rʌsl̩] (v.) 沙沙作響
2   swear [swɛr] (v.) 詛咒；罵髒話
    （動詞三態：swear–swore–sworn）
3   savings [`sevɪŋz] (n.) 積蓄
4   rush [rʌʃ] (v.) 衝
5   go mad 發瘋
6   scatter [`skætɚ] (v.) 散佈

She screamed[1] and turned away. The chair legs came gently but firmly against her back and forced her and Mr Hall out of the room. The door slammed violently and was locked and then suddenly everything was quiet.

Mrs Hall almost fainted[2] on the landing.

"It was spirits[3]!" said Mrs Hall. "Don't let him come in again. I knew he was bad—he put the spirits into my furniture!"

They called the neighbors and told them what happened, and soon a small crowd gathered downstairs, discussing what to do.

Suddenly, upstairs the stranger's door opened. As they looked up in amazement[4], they saw the fully covered figure staring at them with those blue goggles. He came down the stairs slowly, then he entered the sitting room and slammed the door in their faces.

Go Mad

1. "Mad" has two different meanings. What are they?
2. What is the chapter title?
3. How did the furniture go mad?

---

1 scream [skrim] (v.) 尖叫
2 faint [fent] (v.) 昏厥；暈倒
3 spirit [ˈspɪrɪt] (n.) 幽靈
4 amazement [əˈmezmənt] (n.) 吃驚；驚訝

6. The Unveiling[1] of the Stranger

(15) The stranger remained in the sitting room until about midday. People heard him walking up and down, smashing[2] bottles and shouting. He rang the bell three times furiously[3], but no one answered him.

Then the news of the burglary at the vicarage came, and people put two and two together[4]. Mr Hall and a neighbor went to the police station.

It was a beautiful day, and outside people were getting ready for the village fair[5]. Inside the inn, the little group of scared but curious people increased.

Suddenly, the stranger opened his door and stood staring at the people in the bar.

"Mrs Hall!" he called.

Mrs Hall appeared, holding a little tray with an unpaid bill on it.

"Do you want your bill, sir?" she said.

"Why haven't you prepared my meals and answered the bell?"

"Why isn't my bill paid?" said Mrs Hall.

"I told you three days ago I was waiting for a postal payment . . ."

---

1 unveiling [ʌnˈvelɪŋ] (n.) 揭露出來
2 smash [smæʃ] (v.) (n.) 粉碎
3 furiously [ˈfjʊərɪəslɪ] (adv.) 猛烈地
4 put two and two together 根據現有情況推論；綜合判斷
5 village fair 農村市集

"I told you two days ago I wasn't going to wait for any postal payments. You're five days late."

"I told you that my payment hasn't come. Still, I've found some money . . ."

"I wonder where you found it," said Mrs Hall.

That seemed to annoy the stranger very much. "What do you mean?" he asked.

"That I wonder where you found it," said Mrs Hall. "And before I take any bills or get any breakfasts, you have to tell me one or two things. I want to know . . ."

Suddenly the stranger raised his gloved fists and stamped his foot[6]. "Stop!" he shouted with such violence that he silenced her instantly.

"You don't understand," he said, "who I am or what I am. I'll show you."

He put his open hand over his face and then he moved it. The center of his face became a black hole.

"Here," he said, and gave Mrs Hall something.

She held out her hand automatically, but when she saw what she was holding, she screamed loudly and dropped it suddenly. The stranger's nose, pink and shining, was on the floor.

Then he removed his goggles, and everyone in the bar gasped[7]. Then he took off his hat and his bandages.

"Oh, my God!" said someone.

---

6 stamp one's foot 跺腳
7 gasp [gæsp] (v.) 倒抽一口氣

Predict

1. What has happened? Explain in two or three sentences.
2. What do you think will happen now? Make some predictions. Then read the rest of the chapter. Were you right?

Mrs Hall screamed and ran to the door. Everyone ran out. They were prepared for scars[1], disfigurements[2], visible horrors, but nothing! Everyone fell on everyone else, because the man who stood there shouting an incomprehensible[3] explanation had no head.

Everyone in the street ran towards the inn. A crowd quickly gathered and started talking about the headless stranger. They were looking into the inn to try and see him.

Mr Hall and Mr Jaffers, the village policeman, arrived. They went into the sitting room and saw the headless figure, who had bread in one gloved hand and cheese in the other.

"What do you want?" said the stranger.

"Head or no head, mister," said Mr Jaffers, "I'm here to arrest you."

A fight followed, during which the stranger's gloves also came off, and more people joined in.

---

1 scar [skɑr] (n.) 疤；傷痕
2 disfigurement [dɪsˋfɪgjəmənt] (n.) 毀容；外形的損壞
3 incomprehensible [ɪnˌkɑmprɪˋhɛnsəbl̩] (a.) 難懂的；不可思議的

"Stop! I surrender[1]!" cried the stranger. He stood up breathing heavily, headless and handless. "The fact is, I'm all here—head, hands and everything, but I'm invisible. I know it's strange, but it's not a crime. Why do you want to arrest me?"

"The reason why I'm arresting you," said Jaffers, "is not invisibility—it's burglary."

"I'll come," said the stranger, "but no handcuffs[2]."

"I'm sorry, sir, but the rules . . ." said Jaffers.

Suddenly the figure sat down, and the shoes, socks and trousers came off.

"Stop that!" said Jaffers, realizing what was happening. He tried to hold on to the stranger's coat, but it was soon empty in his hand.

"Hold him!" shouted Jaffers. "If he gets the shirt off . . ."

The shirt-sleeve punched[3] Mr Hall's face, and the next minute the shirt was on the floor.

"Hold him!" said everyone, and they all started hitting everybody else, moving towards the door and then down the steps of the inn.

In the street a woman screamed as something pushed her. A dog was kicked and ran away howling[4], and with that, the Invisible Man left Iping.

Hold Him!

- How could you stop the Invisible Man?
  Think of ways with a friend. Share them in class.

7. Mr Thomas Marvel

Mr Thomas Marvel had a large face, a big nose, a wide mouth and a strange beard. He was fat, with short arms and legs. He wore a very old silk hat, and his coat had shoelaces instead of buttons.

He was sitting with his feet in a ditch[5] by the roadside, not far from Iping. He was looking at his old boots and trying on another pair. He didn't know which pair to choose.

"They're just boots," said a Voice.

Marvel looked over his shoulder to reply, but he was amazed to see no one there. He stood up and looked around. Still no one.

"Where are you?" he said. "What's going on?"

"Don't be afraid," said the Voice.

"Where are you?" said Marvel. "Are you dead?"

He was suddenly taken by the neck and shaken violently.

"It's very simple," said the Voice. "I'm an invisible man."

"What?" said Marvel.

---

1 surrender [səˈrɛndɚ] (v.) 投降；屈服
2 handcuffs [ˈhændˌkʌfs] 〔複〕(n.) 手銬
3 punch [pʌntʃ] (v.) 用拳猛擊
4 howl [haʊl] (v.) 嗥叫
5 ditch [dɪtʃ] (n.) 水道

A hand gripped[1] his wrist and made him jump. His fingers touched the hand, went slowly up the arm, and found a bearded face.

"Incredible!" he said. "Invisible—except . . ."

He looked at the empty space more closely. "Have you eaten bread and cheese?" he asked.

"I have, and my body hasn't completely digested[2] them yet. Listen, I need help. I was desperate, and then I saw you and I thought, 'He's an outcast like me.' I want you to help me get clothes and shelter[3] and some other things."

"Oh, I don't know," said Marvel. "This is all too strange for me."

"I've chosen you," said the Voice. "Help me, and I will do great things for you. An invisible man is a man of power. But if you betray[4] me, if you don't do as I say . . ." He paused and hit Marvel's shoulder.

Marvel cried in terror at the touch. "I don't want to betray you," he said. "I'll help you—just tell me what I have to do."

Marvel

1. What do we learn about Marvel's life?
2. What does the Invisible Man want him to do? Talk with a partner.

8. Mr Marvel's Visit to Iping

21 People were enjoying the Whit Monday village fair when Marvel entered Iping. Nobody knew him, but several people noticed him.

From inside his shop opposite[5] the Coach and Horses, Mr Huxter saw him go into the inn and then come out a few minutes later.

Marvel looked around and walked towards the gates of the yard. He stopped at the gate, filled a pipe and started to smoke. Suddenly he put his pipe in his pocket and went into the yard. He reappeared with a big bundle[6] in a blue tablecloth in one hand and three books tied together in the other.

"Stop, thief!" cried Huxter.

Marvel began to run and Huxter set off after him. But after only a few steps he tripped up[7] for no reason and fell face down.

In order to understand what happened, we need to go inside the inn.

---

1 grip [grɪp] (v.) 緊握
2 digest [daɪˋdʒɛst] (v.) 消化
3 shelter [ˋʃɛltɚ] (n.) 躲避處
4 betray [bɪˋtre] (v.) 背叛
5 opposite [ˋɑpəzɪt] (prep.) 在對面
6 bundle [ˋbʌndḷ] (n.) 包裹
7 trip up 絆倒

When Mr Huxter first saw Marvel, Mr Cuss, the village doctor, and Mr Bunting, the vicar, were in the guest sitting room of the Coach and Horses. They were looking at three big books full of incomprehensible symbols and numbers when the door suddenly opened.

A stranger walked in. "Is this the bar?" he asked.

"No," said both gentlemen at once.

"Over the other side," said Mr Bunting.

"Please shut that door," said Mr Cuss.

"All right," said the stranger, in a completely different voice.

Then he spoke in his first voice and said, "Fine. Door closing!" and closed the door.

As the two men sat down to examine the books, they each felt a hand on their necks.

"Where did you learn to read a scientist's private diaries?" said a Voice. The men's heads were banged on the table at the same time.

"Where are my clothes?" The two heads hit the table again.

"Listen," said the Voice. "I could kill you both and get away quite easily if you don't do what I ask. I want clothes and those three books."

Reasons

- Discuss the questions with a partner and give reasons for your answers. What do you think is in the bundle?
- Who is the stranger?
- Why does the Voice want the books?

9. The Invisible Man Loses His Temper [1]

While these things were going on in the sitting room, and while Mr Huxter was watching Marvel smoking his pipe, Mr Hall and Mr Henfrey were in the bar next door. They heard a loud noise, a cry, and then silence.

"Something's wrong," said Mr Hall and knocked on the door.

"Are you all right there?" he asked.

The conversation stopped suddenly, and then started again. Mrs Hall arrived, and the two men were telling her about the first noise when there was another noise.

"Sh!" said Mr Henfrey. "Wasn't that the window?"

Everyone was standing outside the sitting room listening intently when Mr Huxter appeared in the street, shouting "Stop, thief!" At the same time a loud noise came from the sitting room, followed by the sound of windows being closed.

Everyone in the bar rushed out into the street. They saw someone running round the corner holding a parcel, and Mr Huxter flying through the air and landing on his face. Mr Hall and two customers [2] started running after the thief. But after just a few yards, Mr Hall screamed and also went flying, taking one of the customers to the ground with him. The second customer tripped up like all the others.

(24) More people from the village came running round the corner. At first they stopped, astonished[3] to see the lane[4] empty except for the three men on the ground. When they started running again, one by one they fell on top of each other.

Mr Cuss came out of the inn wearing a white sheet round his waist. "Hold him! He's got my trousers! And all of the Vicar's clothes!" he shouted and fell face down on the street.

The village was full of people running and doors slamming, and after a few minutes it was deserted[5]. For two hours nobody found the courage to go out into the street.

Meanwhile[6], Marvel was walking along the road to Bramblehurst, carrying the three books and the big bundle.

"If you try to run away again," said the Voice, "I will kill you."

Tempers

1. What kind of things do people do when they lose their temper?
2. Look at the chapter title. How does the Invisible Man lose his temper?
3. Do you ever lose your temper? Talk with a partner.

---

1 lose one's temper 生氣
2 customer [ˈkʌstəmɚ] (n.) 顧客
3 astonished [əˈstɑnɪʃt] (a.) 驚訝的
4 lane [len] (n.) 巷；車道
5 deserted [dɪˈzɝtɪd] (a.) 廢棄的
6 meanwhile [ˈminˌhwaɪl] (adv.) 其間；同時

10. The Man Who Was Running

(25) It was early evening and Dr Kemp, a tall and slender young man, was sitting in his study on the hill overlooking Port Burdock, doing some important scientific research. As he looked out of the window, he saw a short man in a very old hat running down the hill towards the town.

"Another fool who believes the stories in the newspapers and runs around shouting 'The Invisible Man is coming!'" Dr Kemp thought with contempt[1].

But in Port Burdock, those who saw the terror on Marvel's sweaty face didn't feel contempt. They stopped and stared up and down the road with worried faces. And then something—a wind, a sound like heavy breathing[2]—rushed by.

People screamed, jumped off the pavement, ran into their houses and slammed their doors.

"The Invisible Man's coming!" they shouted.

Inside the Jolly Cricketers pub at the bottom of the hill, the landlord[3], a cab driver, an American man and an off-duty[4] policeman were talking.

"What's the shouting about?" asked the cab driver.

There was the sound of someone running heavily and the door was pushed open violently. Marvel, weeping[5] and disheveled[6], rushed in.

"He's coming!" he screamed in terror. "The Invisible Man! Help! Help!"

"Who's coming? What's going on?" said the policeman, and went to lock the door.

"Help me!" cried Marvel, staggering and weeping, but still gripping the books. "Lock me in somewhere. I ran away. He's going to kill me!"

"You're safe," said the American. "The door's shut. What's it all about?"

A blow[7] suddenly shook the door.

"Hello," cried the policeman, "who's there?"

The landlord helped Marvel hide behind the bar. A window was smashed in, and outside there were sounds of screaming and running. Then everything was quiet.

"Let's unlock the door," said the American, and showed them a small gun. "If he comes in, I'll shoot[8] his legs."

He unlocked the door and took a few steps back.

"Come in," he said.

1 contempt [kən'tɛmpt] (n.) 蔑視
2 breathe [brið] (v.) 呼吸
3 landlord ['lænd,lɔrd] (n.) 老板
4 off-duty [ɔf'djutɪ] (a.) 下班的
5 weep [wip] (v.) 哭泣；哀悼
6 disheveled [dɪ'ʃɛvld] (a.)（頭髮、服裝）凌亂的；不整的
7 blow [blo] (n.) 響聲
8 shoot [ʃut] (v.) 開（槍等）（動詞三態：shoot–shot–shot）

Marvel

🎧▪ What has happened to Marvel so far?
   In pairs make a list.

The door remained closed.

"Are all the other doors locked?" asked Marvel.

"Oh, no!" said the landlord. "The back door!"

He rushed out of the bar and he reappeared after a minute.

"The back door was open!" he said. "He may be inside now!"

Suddenly there was a terrible noise, then a scream, and Marvel was dragged towards the kitchen. The policeman and the cab driver rushed after him. They managed to get hold of the Invisible Man, but they were punched and kicked. However, Marvel ran away, and the men in the kitchen found they were fighting with air.

"Where has the Invisible Man gone?" cried the American. "Outside?"

"This way," said the policeman, going outside.

Stones started to fly towards the men.

"I'll show him!" shouted the American and shot five bullets[1] in the direction of the stones.

A silence[2] followed.

"Get a light," said the policeman. "Let's try to find his body."

Violence

- What violent things does the Invisible Man do and say in this chapter? Think of other violent things he has done or said. Then look back through the book and check.

1 bullet [ˈbʊlɪt] (n.) 子彈；彈丸
2 silence [ˈsaɪləns] (n.) 寂靜；沉默

11. Doctor Kemp's Visitor

28
Dr Kemp heard the shots[1].

About an hour later, the doorbell rang. The servant[2] answered, but she didn't come upstairs to announce[3] a visitor, so he called her.

"Was that a letter?" he asked.

"It was just someone who rang the bell and ran away, sir," she said.

At two o'clock that night Dr Kemp stopped working and went downstairs to his bedroom. As he crossed the hall, he noticed a dark spot on the floor. He touched it—it looked like drying blood. Then he went to his bedroom, but he stopped astonished: there was blood on the handle of his bedroom door.

He went in and heard something moving in the room. Suddenly, he saw a bandage with blood on it, hanging in mid-air. He stared at this in amazement. The bandage was tied around something, but it seemed empty. He tried to touch it, but his hand met invisible fingers. He recoiled[4] at the touch and his face went white.

---

1 shot [ʃɑt] (n.) 發射
2 servant [ˋsɜvənt] (n.) 僕人
3 announce [əˋnauns] (v.) 通報
4 recoil [rɪˋkɔɪl] (v.) 退縮

He looked at the bed. There was blood all over it and the sheets were torn. Then he thought he heard a low voice say, "Kemp!" But Dr Kemp did not believe in voices.

"Stay calm, Kemp. I need help."

"This is impossible," said Kemp. "It's a trick."

The hand gripped Kemp's arm, and the two men fought, but the Invisible Man was stronger and threw Kemp on the floor.

"If you shout, I'll smash your face," the Voice said. "This is no magic. I really am invisible. And I want your help. It's amazing to find you here, Kemp, just by chance. I'm Griffin, of University College. Do you remember me? Medicine student, younger than you, almost an albino[1], tall, with a pink and white face and red eyes. And I have made myself invisible."

"How can a man become invisible?" said Kemp.

"I'm sorry about the blood—it gets visible as it coagulates[2]. Only living tissue[3] can be invisible. I'm starving and cold. Have you got a dressing gown[4] to lend me?"

Kemp gave Griffin his dressing gown and some food. Then he watched the gown take shape and sit on the chair.

He asked Griffin about the shooting, but the man was exhausted[5] and didn't make much sense[6]. He talked about Marvel with long silences between his words.

"That tramp has stolen my books and my money. I could see he wanted to run away . . . Why didn't I kill him!"

"Where did you get the money?" asked Kemp.

"I've had no sleep for nearly three days," said the Invisible Man. "I'm sorry, but I can't tell you tonight. I really must sleep. Don't tell anyone I'm here. Or else . . ."

"I won't. You can have my room."

The Invisible Man checked all the doors and windows to make sure he could escape if he needed to. Then Kemp heard him yawn [7].

Kemp

- What is the connection between the Invisible Man and Kemp?

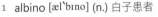

1 albino [ælˈbɪno] (n.) 白子患者
2 coagulate [koˈægjəˌlet] (v.) 使凝結
3 tissue [ˈtɪʃu] (n.) (動、植物的)組織
4 dressing gown 晨袍
5 exhausted [ɪgˈzɔstɪd] (a.) 精疲力竭的
6 doesn't make sense 不合常理
7 yawn [jɔn] (v.) 打哈欠

12. Certain First Principles [1]

Kemp couldn't sleep. He went into his study and found the day's newspapers. He read all the articles about the events in Iping, but none of them mentioned a tramp.

"He's not only invisible," he thought, "but he's mad! Murderous [2]!"

Kemp was still awake at dawn, trying to believe the unbelievable. He told the servants to prepare breakfast for two in the study, and then to stay in the kitchen.

The morning papers arrived and he read about the events at the Jolly Cricketers and a man called Marvel, but there was little information and no mention of the books.

"He's angry," he thought, "and dangerous . . . The things he might do! And he's here . . . What should I do?"

He went to his desk and wrote a note. He addressed the envelope to Colonel Adye, Port Burdock and gave it to his servant to deliver.

Just then Griffin woke up in a bad temper. Kemp heard him smash something in the bedroom, so he went to knock on the door.

"What's the matter?" he asked.

"Nothing," was the answer.

They had breakfast in the study.

"Before we can do anything else, I must understand more about this invisibility," said Kemp, watching food disappear above the headless, handless dressing gown.

"Well," said Griffin, "after London, I moved to Chesilstowe. I left medicine and took up physics to study light. Light fascinated[3] me. An object absorbs[4] light or it reflects[5] or refracts[6] it, or does all these things. If it doesn't reflect or refract or absorb light, then it cannot be visible."

"I know," said Kemp, "But I still don't understand how . . ."

"I discovered a formula[7] for invisibility. It is possible to make a substance refract light in the same way as air does. It then becomes invisible. It's all in the books that tramp has stolen."

Kemp listened in amazement.

---

1 principle ['prɪnsəpl] (n.) 原則；原理
2 murderous ['mɜdərəs] (a.) 蓄意謀殺的
3 fascinate ['fæsn̩ˌet] (v.) 懾住；使著迷
4 absorb [əb'sɔrb] (v.) 吸收
5 reflect [rɪ'flɛkt] (v.) 反射
6 refract [rɪ'frækt] (v.) （使）折射
7 formula ['fɔrmjələ] (n.) 方程式

"I discovered that it's possible to bleach[1] blood and keep all its normal functions. I could also make a living tissue transparent[2]. All except the pigment[3]. And then I realized what this knowledge meant for me, an albino—I could make myself invisible! But after three years of experiments, I found that I couldn't complete my project."

"Why not?"

"I didn't have enough money," said Griffin. "So I robbed my father. The money wasn't his, and he shot himself."

Albino

1. Find the sentence with the word "albino" in it. What is an albino?

2. Why does the Invisible Man want to make himself invisible?

3. Does this change your feelings about him? Discuss with a partner.

1 bleach [blitʃ] (v.) 漂白
2 transparent [træns`pɛrənt] (a.) 透明的
3 pigment [`pɪgmənt] (n.) 色素
4 lodging house 宿舍
5 funeral [`fjunərəl] (n.) 喪禮
6 fabric [`fæbrɪk] (n.) 織品；組織
7 fade [fed] (v.) 褪色；逐漸消失
8 chloroform [`klorə,fɔrm] (n.) 氯仿
9 mist [mɪst] (n.) 薄霧
10 meow [mɪ`au] (v.) 貓叫

13. The House in Great Portland Street

(34) They sat in silence, then Griffin continued his story.

"I moved to London. I rented a large room in a big lodging house[4] in Great Portland Street. I used my father's money to buy the equipment I needed and I built my machine. I worked day and night. The work was nearly finished when my father killed himself. That was last December. I went to the funeral[5] because I had to, but I didn't feel sorry for him—all I could think of was my research."

Kemp listened in silence.

"In my first experiment I put some white wool fabric[6] in my machine. It was the strangest thing in the world to watch the wool fade[7] and disappear. I couldn't believe it myself, but I touched it and it was there. Then I heard a meow behind me, and saw a white cat outside the window."

"And you made her invisible?"

"I made her invisible. I bleached her blood, and I gave her chloroform[8]. Then I bandaged her and put her in the machine. She woke while she was still a mist[9], and meowed[10] loudly and horribly. The old woman from downstairs knocked on the door. Her white cat was all she had. I gave the cat some more chloroform and answered the door. 'Did I hear a cat?' she asked. 'A cat? Not here,' I said, very politely, and I sent her away."

"How long did it take?" asked Kemp.

"Three or four hours. The bones, the tendons[1] and the fat were the last to go. But the colored part in the back of the eyes didn't go. So when she woke up, she was like a ghost— just two eyes moving. She started meowing, very loudly, and of course she was impossible to catch. So I opened the window and finally the meowing moved outside."

"Go on," said Kemp.

"The next day the landlord knocked on my door. He said he knew I spent my nights vivisecting[2] cats and wanted to look at my machine. He wanted to know if I was doing something illegal or dangerous. I lost my temper. I pushed him out, slammed the door and locked it. But this was a problem."

"Why?" asked Kemp.

"I didn't have enough money to move to another house. Invisibility was the only solution. So I took my books and my money and put them in a locker[3] at a post office. Then I made myself invisible."

"Did it hurt?"

"Yes. It was unimaginably painful, but that didn't stop me. I watched my body become like glass, and then the bones, veins and arteries faded. The tendons disappeared last. In the end, I was exhausted. I slept all morning, with my face covered because the light came through my eyelids."

"And then what happened?"

"At about midday the landlord knocked on my door. Very quietly I put the parts of my machine in different places around the room, so that nobody could put it back together. He opened the door and entered with his two sons and the old woman from downstairs. They were amazed to find the room empty. They checked every corner and under the bed, and they were disappointed to find no 'horrors.' When they left, I quietly put all my papers, the bedding and the chair in the middle of the room. Then I lit a fire with some matches, and left."

1 tendon ['tɛndən] (n.)〔解剖〕腱
2 vivisect [ˌvɪvə'sɛkt] (n.) 活體解剖
3 locker ['lɑkɚ] (n.) 寄物鎖櫃；衣物櫃

(37) "You set the house on fire!" exclaimed[1] Kemp.

"It was the only way to cover my tracks[2]. I left quietly and went out into the street. I was invisible. I started planning all the things I could now do with no fear of punishment[3]. It was great. I felt like a man who could see in a city of the blind. But soon I realized there were problems. I could avoid people coming towards me, but not people behind me. And crowds were dangerous for me."

"Ah! If people can't see you, they'll think there's nothing there . . ."

"Exactly. I started walking in the gutter[4]. It hurt my feet because it was rougher than the pavement and I had to keep jumping out of the way of the traffic. And, without clothes, I was very cold, because it was January, and the mud[5] on the road was freezing. Then I discovered that dogs could smell me. I had to run when one started chasing me and barking."

"What an impossible situation!"

"I ran for a while before I realized that the road was too crowded. I couldn't go back because of the dog. So I ran up the steps of a house and stood there waiting. The dog turned around and ran away."

"Go on," said Kemp.

1 exclaim [ɪksˋklem] (v.) 驚呼
2 cover one's tracks 掩蓋行蹤
3 punishment [ˋpʌnɪʃmənt] (n.) 懲罰
4 gutter [ˋgʌtɚ] (n.) 排水溝
5 mud [mʌd] (n.) 泥巴

"Then two boys stopped near me. 'Can you see them?' said one. 'See what?' said the other. 'Those footprints[1] of bare feet.' I looked down and saw they were looking at my footprints on the white steps. 'A barefooted man went up those steps and didn't come down,' said one. 'And his foot was bleeding[2].' And then he pointed at my feet, and I realized that splashes of mud showed the shape of my feet. 'Look!' he said. 'It's like the ghost of a foot!' and he moved to touch my feet."

"What did you do?"

"I stamped my foot. The boy jumped back in surprise and I jumped onto the steps of the next house. But the other boy followed the movement. He started shouting, 'Feet! Look! Feet running!' I ran and ran until my feet got hot and dry and stopped leaving footprints."

Problems

1. What problems does the Invisible Man have now that he is invisible?

2. Would you like to be invisible? Talk with a partner.

1 footprint [ˈfʊt‚prɪnt] (n.) 腳印
2 bleed [blid] (v.) 流血 (動詞三態：bleed–bled–bled)
3 approach [əˈprotʃ] (v.) 接近

(39) "I was tired, hungry, miserable, cold and in pain, and then I realized that a snow storm was approaching[3]! Suddenly I had an idea. I went to Omniums, the big store where you can buy everything, from food to paintings. I found a quiet area in an upper floor and I hid, waiting for closing time. When the cleaners left, I was alone in the huge store. I took all the clothes I needed, some money and food. Then I went to sleep in the beds department."

"Go on," said Kemp.

"I woke up suddenly and saw two shop assistants approaching. They saw me and they started chasing me. I got away a few times and then the police arrived. I realized that the only way I could get out of there was by being invisible. So I took my clothes off and left. I began to realize the problem. I had no shelter and no clothes. If I wore clothes, I lost all my advantage. Even eating was impossible, because before the food is fully digested, it's visible."

"I never thought of that," said Kemp.

"Nor had I. And there were other dangers. Snow, rain, fog and dust make my outline visible—I wasn't going to remain invisible for long. Then I remembered that there are shops that sell theatrical[1] costumes[2]."

"Good idea!" said Kemp.

"I found an old-fashioned, dark theatrical shop, with a dark house above it, in Drury Lane. There was no one inside and I entered. As I opened the door, a bell rang. So I left the door open and hid, waiting for someone to turn up. A short, thin man, hunched[3], with thick, dark eyebrows, long arms and very short bandy[4] legs came through the back door. 'Those boys again!' he said. He closed the front door and went to the back door. I moved to follow him but he heard me and stopped. He went out of the back door quickly and slammed it in my face."

"Why did you want to go into the house?" asked Kemp.

"Because there was nothing I could use in the shop, and I hoped he had more in the house. He came back to check the shop and he left the door open, so I went inside. I found myself in a little room with another closed door to the house upstairs. I waited until he came back and opened the door. Then I slipped[5] behind him as he went upstairs. He stopped suddenly, listening, and I very nearly walked into him."

"That man's hearing was incredible!" said Kemp.

---

1 theatrical [θɪ`ætrɪkl̩] (a.) 劇場的
2 costume [`kɑstjum] (n.) 戲裝
3 hunched [hʌntʃt] (a.) 弓著身子的
4 bandy [`bændɪ] (a.) 向外彎的
5 slip [slɪp] (v.) 悄悄走；溜走；滑動

"It was. He kept going in and out of rooms, slamming the doors before I could follow him. The house was very old, with rats everywhere. I managed to[1] get into a room full of clothes, but he heard me and came in holding a small gun. He looked around, walked out and locked the door. I made a noise to make him come back, and when he did, I knocked him on the head with a chair. Then I gagged[2] him and tied him up."

"You left him tied up?"

"I had to. Then I searched the whole house, and I found what I needed—a false nose, goggles, a wig[3], clothes and shoes. I also found some money. I checked myself in a mirror—I looked strange, of course, but not impossible. So I walked out into the street, and no one seemed to notice me."

"What happened next?," asked Kemp, glancing out of the window.

"Well, I realized that I couldn't eat in public without revealing[4] my invisible face. And when I thought about it more, Kemp, I realized it was stupid and crazy to be an Invisible Man. I thought about all the things most people want. It's true that invisibility made it possible to get them— but it also made it impossible to enjoy them."

1 manage to 成功設法
2 gag [gæg] (v.) 塞住……的口
3 wig [wɪg] (n.) 假髮
4 reveal [rɪ'vil] (v.) 顯露出

(42) But why did you go to Iping?" said Kemp, anxious[1] to keep Griffin talking.

"I went there to work. To find a way of undoing my invisibility, after I have done everything I plan to do. And that is what I want to talk to you about now."

Realization

1. What important thing does the Invisible Man realize?
2. What reasons does he give?
3. What does he want now?
4. How do you feel about him? Say why.

---

1 anxious [ˈæŋkʃəs] (a.) 焦慮的
2 fail [fel] (v.) 失敗
3 glance [glæns] (v.) 一瞥；掃視
4 reign of terror 恐怖統治
5 terrify [ˈtɛrəˌfaɪ] (v.) 使害怕
6 dominate [ˈdɑməˌnet] (v.) 支配；控制
7 disobey [ˌdɪsəˈbe] (v.) 不服從；違抗

15. The Plan That Failed[2]

Kemp glanced[3] out of the window and saw three men approaching the house. He stood up so that Griffin couldn't see them.

"So what's your plan now?" he asked.

"I need to get my books from that tramp. Do you know where he is?"

"He's in the town police station, by his own request," said Kemp, a little nervously, hearing footsteps outside.

"My mistake," said Griffin, "was to think I could do this alone. I need a partner and a hiding place where I can sleep, eat and rest."

"Go on," said Kemp, listening for any kind of movement in the house.

"I've realized that invisibility is only useful for getting away from people and for approaching them. Therefore it's particularly useful for killing. I can walk round an armed man, kill him and escape. And it is killing we must do."

"Why killing?" asked Kemp.

"The only way to use my invisibility to our advantage is by starting a Reign of Terror[4]. The Invisible Man must terrify[5] and dominate[6] towns like Port Burdock. He must give his orders, and kill everyone who disobeys[7] and also those who help them."

Terror

1. What does the Invisible Man want to do?
2. How can he terrify people?
3. What terrifies you?

Kemp was listening to the sound of his front door opening and closing.

"But your partner would be in a difficult position," said Kemp.

"Nobody would know he was a partner," said Griffin. And then suddenly, "Sh! What's that downstairs?"

"Nothing," said Kemp, suddenly beginning to speak loud and fast. "I don't agree with this, Griffin. Why do you want to play a game against humanity[1]? How can you hope to find happiness? Don't do it. Instead, publish your results and . . ."

Griffin interrupted him "Somebody's downstairs," he whispered[2].

"You're imagining it," said Kemp.

---

1 humanity [hjuˈmænətɪ] (n.) 人性；人道
2 whisper [ˈhwɪspɚ] (v.) 低聲說

"Let me see," said Griffin, and moved towards the door.

And then things happened very quickly. Kemp moved to stop Griffin. Griffin was surprised for a second, and cried, "Traitor[1]!" Suddenly the dressing gown opened.

Kemp ran out of the room and slammed the door. He tried to lock it but the key fell on the floor. Then he tried to hold the door shut but Griffin managed to open it. Invisible fingers gripped Kemp's throat and he let go of the door handle to defend himself. Griffin pushed the door wide open and Kemp fell on the floor.

Colonel Adye, the recipient[2] of Kemp's letter, was the chief of the Port Burdock police. He was halfway up the stairs when Kemp suddenly appeared, fighting against a door and falling over. Adye was struck violently—by nothing—and fell down the stairs. He heard the two police officers in the hall shout and run. The front door slammed violently.

Kemp staggered down the stairs, disheveled and with his lip bleeding.

"He's gone! God help us!" he cried.

1   traitor ['tretɚ] (n.) 叛徒
2   recipient [rɪ'sɪpɪənt] (n.) 收受者；接受者
3   hunt [hʌnt] (v.) 追捕
4   inhuman [ɪn'hjumən] (a.) 無人性的
5   injure ['ɪndʒɚ] (v.) 傷害
6   alert [ə'lɝt] (n.) 警戒
7   weapon ['wɛpən] (n.) 武器

16. The Hunting[3] of the Invisible Man

"He's mad," said Kemp. "Inhuman[4] and completely selfish. He only thinks of himself. He has injured[5] people and he'll kill people unless we stop him."

"We must catch him," said Adye. "But how?"

"You must use all your men," said Kemp. "Prevent him from leaving this area. Watch all trains and roads and shipping. He wants to get some notebooks that are important to him from a man in your police station. A man called Marvel."

"I know," said Adye. "But the tramp says he hasn't got the books."

"He thinks the tramp has them. And you must prevent him from eating or sleeping, day and night. Everybody in the area must be on alert[6]. Lock up all food. People must lock up their houses. The whole area must start hunting for him. Use dogs. They can smell him and he's scared of them."

"Good," said Adye. "What else?"

"After eating, his food shows until his body has digested it. So he has to hide after eating. Keep checking everywhere. And hide all weapons[7]. He can't carry any weapon for long without revealing himself, but if he's near someone, he can find something and kill them."

"I'll go and organize everything," said Adye.

It was all done with incredible speed. Before two o'clock it was still possible for the Invisible Man to leave the area, but after two it became impossible. All transportation was on high alert. And in the area of twenty miles around Port Burdock, men armed with guns and sticks went out in groups of three or four, with dogs, to search the roads and fields.

The Police

- What do the police want to do?

Mounted policemen[1] rode through the countryside, stopping at every house and warning people to lock their doors and windows. All the schools closed and the children were sent home. But that evening people in the area were horrified by the news of the murder of Mr Wicksteed.

Mr Wicksteed was a quiet man of forty-five or forty-six. The last person to see him alive was a girl walking through a field. She said he looked as if he was trying to reach for something, but she couldn't see what. Madness seemed the only explanation for the murder. The Invisible Man attacked a harmless man with an iron bar[2]. He broke his arm and smashed his head to jelly.

---

1 mounted policeman 騎警
2 bar [bɑr] (n.) 棒子；酒吧

17. The Siege[3] of Kemp's House

 The next day Kemp received the following letter:

> *Today is the first day of Terror. Port Burdock is no longer under the Queen. It is under me. This is Day One of Year One of the new age[4]—the Age of the Invisible Man. There will be one execution[5] to set an example—a man named Kemp. Don't help him, my people, or Death will come for you also. Today Kemp will die.*

Kemp called his servants and told them to check that all the doors and windows were locked and to close all the shutters[6]. From a drawer in his bedroom he took a small gun and put it in his pocket. He wrote a note to Adye, and gave it to his servant to deliver.

---

3 siege [sidʒ] (n.) 圍攻
4 new age 新世紀
5 execution [ˌɛksɪˈkjuʃən] (n.) 處決；執行
6 shutters [ˈʃʌtəz] (n.) 〔複〕百葉窗；百葉遮簾

"There's no danger to you," he said.

"We will catch him!" he thought. "And I am the bait[1]."

Suddenly he heard the front doorbell. It was Adye.

"The Invisible Man has attacked your servant!" he said. "A note from you was snatched[2] out of her hand. He's near here. What was the note about?"

Kemp gave Adye the Invisible Man's letter.

"I suggested setting a trap[3] in my note," said Kemp. "But like a fool, I sent the note out with my servant."

There was a loud noise of smashing glass from upstairs.

"It's a window!" shouted Kemp. Another smashing sound followed.

"He's going to do the whole house," said Kemp. "But he's a fool. The shutters are up and the glass will fall outside. He'll cut his feet."

"Have you got a gun?" asked Adye.

"Yes, but only one. It has five bullets in it."

"Give it to me. I'll go to the police station and get the dogs. I'll bring it back," said Adye. "You'll be safe here."

Kemp gave him the gun and went to the door. He unlocked it as silently as possible.

Adye went out quickly and was near the gate when a Voice said, "Stop!"

Adye stopped.

"Where are you going?" said the Voice.

---

1 bait [bet] (n.) 誘餌；圈套
2 snatch [snætʃ] (v.) 奪走；搶奪
3 trap [træp] (n.) 陷阱；圈套

50

"Where I go," Adye said slowly, "is my own business."

The words were still on his lips when he was hit and fell backwards. He drew his gun and fired, but the weapon was taken from his hand.

The Voice laughed. Adye saw the gun in mid-air above him.

"Get up," said the Voice. "Don't try any games and go back to the house."

Kemp was in his study, crouching⁴ among the broken glass and peering⁵ over the edge of the window sill⁶.

He saw Adye talking. "Why doesn't he fire?" he thought.

Then the gun moved a little, and Kemp realized that the Invisible Man was holding it.

Adye turned and walked towards the house, with the gun following him. Then things happened very quickly. Adye turned around. He tried to grab the gun and missed it. Then he threw up his hands and fell forward on his face, leaving smoke in the air. Kemp did not hear the shot.

There was a loud knocking at the front door. Kemp armed himself with a poker and went to check that all the windows on the ground floor were locked. Everything was safe and quiet.

He returned to his study. Adye lay in the garden, but Kemp saw his servant and two policemen coming towards the house.

---

4 crouch [kraʊtʃ] (v.) 蹲伏；蜷伏
5 peer [pɪr] (v.) 凝視；盯著看
6 window sill 窗沿

85

Suddenly he heard heavy blows and the sound of wood breaking. Kemp followed the noise and opened the kitchen door just as the broken shutters came flying into the kitchen.

"He's found the axe!" he thought.

And then he saw the gun pointing at him through the broken shutter. He moved back, and the Invisible Man fired a shot but missed him.

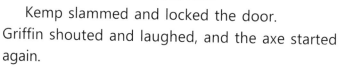

Kemp slammed and locked the door. Griffin shouted and laughed, and the axe started again.

"He'll be inside any moment now," he thought. "This door won't keep him out for long."

The front doorbell rang again. It was his servant and the two policemen. Kemp quickly let them in and locked the door again.

"The Invisible Man!" said Kemp. "He has a gun with two shots left. He's in the kitchen—or will be soon. He's found an axe. And he's killed Adye."

Adye

1. Why does he leave the house?
2. How many shots does he fire?
3. What happens to him?

Suddenly they heard blows on the kitchen door and then the door opening.

"This way," said Kemp, and led the men into the dining room.

Kemp handed the dining-room poker to one policeman and the one he was carrying to the other. The axe and the gun appeared.

The gun fired its penultimate[1] shot and tore[2] a painting. One of the policemen hit the gun with his poker and sent it to the floor. The axe hit him on the head and he fell, but fortunately he was wearing a helmet. The second policeman, aiming behind the axe, hit something soft that snapped[3]. There was a cry of pain and the axe fell to the ground. The policeman put his foot on the axe and struck again. Then he stood holding the poker, listening.

He heard the dining-room window open and the sound of running feet. The first policeman sat up, with blood running down between his eye and ear.

"Where is he?"

"Don't know. I've hit him. He may still be here."

Suddenly they heard the sound of bare feet on the kitchen floor.

"He's escaped through the back door!" said the first policeman.

---

1 penultimate [pɪˈnʌltəmɪt] (a.) 倒數第二的
2 tear [tɛr] (v.) 扯破；撕掉（動詞三態：tear–tore–torn）
3 snap [snæp] (v.) 突然斷掉

They went into the dining room.

"Doctor Kemp . . ." one of the policeman began and then stopped.

The dining-room window was wide open, and there was no sign of Dr Kemp.

Weapons

1. What weapons does the Invisible Man use?
2. How does he get them?
3. What does he do with them?

18. The Hunter Hunted

Kemp ran towards the town. The road was deserted and the distance seemed endless. He could hear the sound of footsteps behind him. He was terrified.

As he entered the town, he could see heaps of gravel[1] by the road. He passed the door of the Jolly Cricketers and saw a tram driver staring at him and the astonished faces of road workers peering above the gravel.

"The Invisible Man!" he cried to the workers, pointing vaguely behind him. Then he turned into a little side street, then turned again. He ran back into the main street, trying to attract as much attention as he could.

He looked up the street and saw a huge road worker running towards him carrying a spade[2], followed by the tram driver and other men. Men and women were running towards him from the other direction too, some carrying sticks. Kemp stopped, breathing heavily.

"He's near here!" he cried. "Form a line across . . ."

---

1 gravel [ˈɡrævl] (n.) 砂礫；碎石
2 spade [sped] (n.) 鏟子

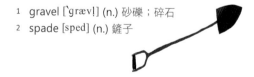

Think

🔊 ▪ What happens next? Share your ideas with a friend.

(54) Suddenly he was hit hard under the ear. He managed to stay on his feet and he struck a blow that hit nothing. Then he was hit again and fell on the ground. He felt a knee on his stomach. Two hands gripped his throat, one with a weaker grip than the other.

He gripped the wrists and heard a cry of pain. Then the spade of the road worker came down through the air and struck with a thud[1]. He felt a drop of something on his face. The grip on his throat suddenly relaxed, and with a huge effort Kemp got on top of the Invisible Man. He gripped the unseen elbows near the ground.

"I've got him!" screamed Kemp. "Help! He's down! Hold his feet!"

After that, the only sounds were of blows, kicks and heavy breathing.

The Invisible Man tried to fight back, but Kemp didn't let him go. Then suddenly there was a wild scream of "Mercy[2]! Mercy!" and a choking[3] sound.

"Get back," cried Kemp. "He's hurt. Stand back!"People moved away, and Kemp, with his face bruised[4] and his lips bleeding, seemed to examine the air.

"His mouth's all wet," he said.

And then, "Good God! He's not breathing. I can't feel his heart!"

Suddenly an old woman screamed and pointed. And looking where she pointed, everyone saw veins, arteries, bones and tendons and the outline of a transparent hand.

"There are his feet!" cried a policeman.

Slowly, beginning at his hands and feet, the strange change continued. The tendons appeared, then the bones, veins and arteries, then the flesh and skin. At first the body resembled a mist and then it quickly became dense[5] and opaque[6]. Now they could see his battered[7] chest and face.

When at last the crowd moved away for Kemp to stand up, the bruised and broken body of a young man of about thirty lay on the ground. His hair and beard were albino-white, his eyes were wide open and like red glass, and he looked angry and distressed[8].

1 thud [θʌd] (n.) 砰的一聲；重擊聲
2 mercy [ˋmɝsɪ] (n.) 慈悲；仁慈
3 choking [ˋtʃokɪŋ] (a.) 哽噎的；窒息的
4 bruised [bruzd] (a.) 瘀青的
5 dense [dɛns] (a.) 濃密的
6 opaque [oˋpek] (a.) 不透明的
7 battered [ˋbætɚd] (a.) 打扁了的
8 distressed [dɪˋstrɛst] (a.) 痛苦的

"Cover him!" said a man. "For God's sake, cover that face!"

Someone brought a sheet and they carried the body into the Jolly Cricketers. It was there that Griffin, the most brilliant physicist the world has ever seen, ended his strange and terrible career.

Kemp

- Imagine you are Kemp. What would you say about the Invisible Man to a friend? Talk with a partner.

The Epilogue [1]

If you want to learn more about the story, you must go to the Invisible Man, a little inn near Port Burdock. The landlord is a fat man with short arms and legs and a big nose. He will tell you what happened to him after the death of the Invisible Man. The magistrate [2] tried to take away the money they found on him. But they couldn't prove whose money it was, so they had to give up [3].

And if you want to stop his stories, ask him about the three books. He admits he had them, but says that the Invisible Man took them. And then he leaves the bar.

And every night, when the inn is closed, he unlocks a cupboard and then a drawer in the cupboard. He takes out three books, puts them on the table and tries to study them.

"How clever he was!" he thinks. "When I can understand these, I won't do what he did. I'll just . . . well . . ."

Then he goes into a dream, the wonderful dream of his life.

---

1 epilogue [ˈɛpəˌlɔg] (n.) 結尾；尾聲
2 magistrate [ˈmædʒɪsˌtret] (n.) 地方法官
3 give up 放棄

95

The Landlord

1. Who is the landlord?
2. Who did the money really belong to?
3. What do you think happens in the landlord's dream? Talk with a partner.

After Reading

1 ▶ Talk About the Story

1 Answer the questions.

a) Did you enjoy reading the story? Why/Why not?

b) In your opinion, was Griffin interesting as a character? Say why/why not.

c) Do you think H. G. Wells intended the other characters to be interesting? Say why/why not.

d) Do you think there is a hero in this story? If you do, who is it, and why?

e) Which is the best part of the story? Why?

f) Imagine you are Dr Kemp: Would you do what he did?

g) Do you think the characters' reactions to Griffin's invisibility are realistic?

h) Do you think Griffin's development is realistic?

i) Would you like to see a film version of *The Invisible Man*?

j) Imagine you are the director of the film version of the story: Which famous actors would you cast as Griffin and Dr Kemp? Why?

2 Share your ideas with the class.

3 Work in small groups. Make a list of films or stories you know in which:

a) a scientific experiment is carried out with no consideration for the consequences.

[b] the main character loses control and becomes increasingly dangerous.

[c] someone is killed when their dream comes true.

[4] Compare your group's lists with the other groups' lists. Did anybody include the same films or stories?

2 Comprehension

[1] Read the sentences and tick (✓) true (T) or false (F). Correct the false sentences.

T F [a] Iping is an important town that attracts a lot of tourists.

T F [b] Griffin becomes part of the community in Iping.

T F [c] Griffin has a lot of money.

T F [d] It is difficult for people in Iping to trust Griffin.

T F [e] Whit Monday is a big community event in Iping.

T F [f] Mr Marvel is happy to help Griffin.

T F [g] Griffin learns that invisibility has fewer advantages than he thought.

T F [h] Griffin cannot carry anything without revealing his presence.

T F [i] Griffin wants to use his invisibility to become rich and then become visible again.

T F [j] Griffin thinks Kemp will help him because they are both scientists.

◀ **2** Work with a partner and explain the part that the following things play in the story.

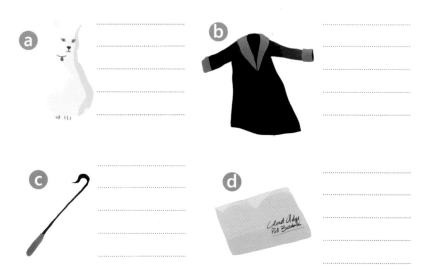

a

b

c

d

3 Tick (✓) all the things that can reveal Griffin's presence when he's alive and naked.

☐ snow   ☐ breathing

☐ his shadow   ☐ his hair

☐ rain   ☐ sneezing

☐ fog   ☐ dust

☐ his eyes   ☐ undigested food in his stomach

☐ his strength   ☐ the blood in his veins

☐ dogs   ☐ his footprints

4 Read the text and answer the questions.
Then share your answers with the class.

A calendar year is 365 days, but the Earth takes 365 ¼ days to revolve around the Sun. So every four years a day is added to the calendar. The extra day, called Leap Day, is February 29th, and the year is called a Leap Year. Hundreds of years ago, the Leap Day was not recognized in British law. As the day had no legal status, people decided they were allowed break from tradition on that day so, for example, it is the day in which women can propose marriage to men. There are many myths about the Leap Year in different countries: It's considered very unlucky in some, very lucky in others, bad for farming, and bad for getting married, and some people believe that more people die in a Leap Year than in other years.

a The story begins with Griffin's arrival in Iping during a snow storm on February 29th. What is Wells telling us by choosing that date?

b Are there any traditions or myths about the Leap Year in your country? If so, what are they?

c Do you know anybody who was born on February 29th? If so, when do they celebrate their birthday in non-leap years?

3 ⟩ Characters

1 Answer the questions.

a) Which character is very intelligent, decisive and brave?

b) Which character is the first to be hit by an invisible fist, but is too shocked to tell the others?

c) Which character kills himself?

d) Which characters see some bloody footprints?

e) Which character is the first person to fight Griffin?

f) Whose house does Griffin set on fire?

g) Which character pretends to be Griffin's friend?

h) Who is Griffin's last victim?

i) Which character doesn't trust Griffin from the start?

j) Who has their only companion taken away by Griffin?

k) Which character is robbed and imprisoned in their own house?

l) Who is shot and killed by Griffin?

m) Which two characters investigate Griffin's room at the Coach and Horses?

n) Who benefits from the events in the story?

2 Answer the questions below. Write about 50 words for each one giving reasons for your answers.

GRIFFIN   KEMP   ADYE

a In what ways are Griffin and Kemp similar?

b In what ways are they different?

c In what ways are Kemp and Adye similar?

3 Read the sentences and tick (✓) T (true) or F (false).

T **F** a Adye walks back to the house with a gun following him.

T **F** b Mr Bunting goes down the stairs holding an axe.

T **F** c Mr Marvel studies Kemp's books secretly.

T **F** d The landlord in Great Portland Street doesn't trust Griffin and thinks he's a burglar.

T **F** e Mr Huxter is the first person who is tripped up by Griffin when Marvel runs off with the bundle.

T **F** f Mr Jaffers tries to arrest the Invisible Man for burglary.

T **F** g The American shoots at the Invisible Man to protect Kemp.

T **F** h Mr Henfrey notices that the stranger hasn't given his name.

T **F** i Kemp finds mud all over his bed.

T **F** j At first, Mrs Hall is worried the stranger may be ill.

4 Correct the sentences in Exercise **3** that are false.

5 Discuss these questions about Griffin with a partner.

a Why did Griffin study light?

b Why did Griffin make himself invisible?

c What is Griffin trying to do in Iping?

d What problems does Griffin have when he is invisible?

e What kind of help does Griffin want from Mr Marvel?

f What kind of help does Griffin want from Dr Kemp?

g Does Griffin change during the story, and if so, in what ways and why?

4 Vocabulary

1 Match the words to the definitions.
Two words have the same definition.

_____ a cry

_____ b whisper

_____ c muffle

_____ d rave

_____ e shout

_____ f scream

_____ g howl

_____ h exclaim

1 to talk in a very angry, uncontrolled way

2 to say something very loudly

3 to make a loud, high sound because you are in pain, frightened or angry

4 to make a long, loud sound like a dog, usually to express pain or sadness

5 say in a surprised way

6 to speak very quietly, using the breath but not the voice

7 to make a quiet, less clear sound

2 Complete the sentences with the correct form of the verbs in Exercise **1**. There can be more than one answer.

[a] Mrs Bunting was woken by a noise. She woke her husband and softly _____, "I think there's somebody downstairs."

[b] He had a hand over his mouth, so his voice was _____.

[c] The strange man _____ for hours about his many problems.

[d] People were so frightened that they _____ and ran away.

[e] Last night someone was _____ like a wolf in the fields near Port Burdock.

[f] "You set the house on fire!" _____ Kemp.

[g] When Griffin realized what was going on, he looked at Dr Kemp and angrily _____, "Traitor!"

[h] As he ran towards the road workers and the crowd in the street, Dr Kemp _____ "The Invisible Man!" so that everybody could hear him.

3 Circle the word in each group that is different to the others. Explain why to a friend.

[a] stranger	traitor	bandage	landlord
[b] crouch	tramp	punch	rush
[c] poker	injure	axe	spade
[d] gagged	exhausted	distressed	irritated
[e] yawn	sneeze	shoot	gasp

4 Answer the questions using a word in Exercise **3**.

_____ ⓐ What might you do when you're very surprised by something?

_____ ⓑ What might you do if you've got a cold?

_____ ⓒ If you're injured and have a wound, what is usually put on it?

_____ ⓓ What do you use to dig in the ground?

_____ ⓔ What might you do if you're exhausted?

_____ ⓕ What might you do if a stranger attacks you in the street?

_____ ⓖ If someone betrays their country, what are they?

5 Look at the pictures below. Write your own definitions for the objects.

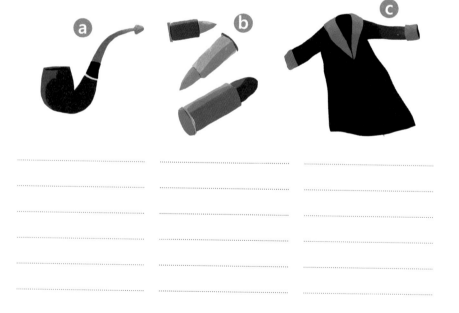

....

....

....

....

....

....

5 Language

1 Rewrite the following sentences using the words given and the active form.

a All his head above his blue goggles was covered by a white bandage. *(A white bandage)*

_____

_____

b Mr Hall was struck violently in the chest and thrown out of the room. *(Somebody)*

_____

_____

c The door was slammed in Mr Hall's face and locked. *(Somebody)*

_____

d Griffin's books weren't understood by anyone. *(No one)*

_____

e Once or twice things were broken with sudden violence. *(Once or twice the stranger)*

_____

f A match was struck and the study was filled with yellow light. *(Somebody/yellow light)*

_____

g Suddenly he was hit hard under the ear. *(Somebody)*

_____

h Marvel was suddenly taken by the neck and shaken violently. *(The Invisible Man)*

_____

2 Rewrite the following sentences using the passive form. Use "by" only when necessary.

(a) The shirt-sleeve punched Mr Hall's face.

_____

(b) Two shop assistants chased Griffin around the store.

_____

(c) Did people search the roads and fields all day?

_____

(d) A blow suddenly shook the door.

_____

(e) The Invisible Man tripped up three men and they fell on the ground.

_____

(f) Someone struck him violently in the chest.

_____

(g) How many people did Griffin attack and kill?

_____

(h) The servant didn't deliver Kemp's note to Colonel Adye.

_____

3 Work with a partner. Explain the difference in meaning between these two sentences. Which is the first conditional? Which is the second conditional?

(a) If the Invisible Man finds Marvel, the tramp will be terrified.

(b) If the Invisible Man found Marvel, the tramp would be terrified.

4 Read the situations. Decide how likely they are to happen. Then write sentences using either the first or second conditional.

[a] You find $500,000 under your bed.

If I _____

[b] You eat too much tomorrow.

[c] Your best friend rings you this evening.

[d] You wake up and find you are a monkey.

[e] There's a big fire in the building next door.

[f] You go to bed late at the weekend.

5 Read these sentences. Underline the relative pronouns and circle the words they refer to.

[a] The only light in the room was from the fire, which lit his goggles but left the rest of his face in darkness.

[b] He had an enormous mouth that filled the lower half of his face.

[c] They heard the sound of rustling paper again—it was the savings that the vicar kept in the drawer.

[d] A stranger in a large hat that hid his face walked in.

[e] The man who stood there shouting an incomprehensible explanation had no head.

[f] "I'll show him," shouted the American, and shot five bullets in the direction which the stones were coming from.

[g] "It's all in the books that the tramp has stolen."

6 Plot and Theme

1 Put Griffin's actions in the order in which he did them.
Write the letters in the first row of boxes.

	1	2	3	4	5	6	7	8	9	10	11	12	13
Ex 1													
Ex 2													

[a] Robbed the shopkeeper and left him tied and gagged in his house.

[b] Discovered a formula for invisibility.

[c] Attacked Kemp's house and killed Colonel Adye.

[d] Tried to kill Marvel.

[e] Made himself invisible.

[f] Took the old woman's cat and experimented with it.

[g] Took up physics to study light.

[h] Murdered Mr Wicksteed.

[i] Robbed his father and didn't feel guilty about it.

[j] Set the lodging house on fire.

[k] Chased Kemp and tried to kill him.

[l] Robbed Iping's vicar.

[m] Forced Marvel to help him.

2 Now put Griffin's actions on the order in which they are told in the story. Write the letters in the second row of boxes.

3 Look at the numbers for each action and answer the questions.

ⓐ Are they the same for each action?

ⓑ Did the author tell the story in chronological order?

ⓒ What did the author do?

ⓓ What is the effect of the author's choice?

4 Read the text and answer the questions.

H. G. Wells believed that a science fiction story should contain only one single "magic," fantastic and extraordinary element. He wrote that, "As soon as the magic trick has been done, the whole business of the fantasy writer is to keep everything else human and real."

a) Which extraordinary element or elements are in *The Invisible Man*?

b) Is everything else in the story human and real? If not, what is not realistic?

c) Can you give two examples of something human and real in the story?

d) Did H. G. Wells follow his own rules in *The Invisible Man*? If not, in what ways did he break them?

5 What are the themes of the story? Read the sentences and tick (✓) the ones that apply.

- ☐ a Scientists must always think about the consequences of their work and actions.
- ☐ b People may use science for evil purposes.
- ☐ c It is important to believe in yourself.
- ☐ d Scientific advances can have bad results as well as good results.
- ☐ e Society is changing fast.
- ☐ f It is possible for society to lose control of its scientific and technological achievements.
- ☐ g Scientists must not try to gain a personal advantage from their discoveries.
- ☐ h Society should be able to say yes or no to new technology.

6 Discuss your answers to Exercise **5** with a partner. Which themes do you most agree with? Why?

The Luddite Rebellion

Today, the word Luddite is generally used to mean someone who is too old-fashioned to like and use technological innovations. However, the origins of the word mark the beginning of a conflict[1] that started with the Industrial Revolution[2] and continues today.

The Luddites were a social movement[3] which started in the British Midlands in 1811. The name comes from a probably fictional story about a young worker called Ned Ludd, who smashed a textile[4] machine. The Luddites were skilled textile workers who, during the Industrial Revolution, found themselves unable to earn a living and feed their families.

AT WORK

Luddite [ˈlʌdaɪt]

noun [C]

a person who is opposed to new technology or ways of working

1 conflict [ˈkɑnflɪkt] (n.) 衝突
2 Industrial Revolution 工業革命
3 movement [ˈmuvmənt] (n.) 運動
4 textile [ˈtɛkstaɪl] (a.) 紡織的

This was because industrialists and factory owners were replacing the skilled workers with machines that could be operated by cheap unskilled workers. The result was that skilled workers became unemployed and unskilled workers worked long hours for very low pay, while the industrialists became increasingly rich.

The Luddites organized protests and often smashed the machines. In fact, they weren't against the machines. They wanted better pay and skilled workers to work the machines. Their movement was so strong and so many people supported them that the army was sent to stop the rebellion[1]. After a trial in the city of York in 1813, seventeen men were executed[2].

The Age of Robots

Since then, the desire to maximize[3] profits has encouraged the invention of technologies that speed up production and reduce the need to use people to do work.

In developed countries, some of this technological innovation has become part of a lot of people's everyday lives—most of us cannot imagine our lives without our smartphones, tablets and home computers. In other words, society has accepted these things by buying them.

However, the digital revolution is also having other effects. As more and more jobs are done by robots, fewer and fewer people are needed to operate the machines. And the jobs that are taken by robots are not being replaced by other "human" jobs. In other words, there are fewer jobs in general.

Now, in the twenty-first century, we are entering a new phase of automation [4]. Driverless cars, robots and delivery drones are increasingly replacing people in the transport and distribution industries. Will workers protest against automation as they have done in the past? Or will new technology bring more advantages than disadvantages?

- Look at your answers to Exercise 5 on page 113.
  Are any of the themes relevant to the Luddite Rebellion?

- Are any of the themes relevant to the automation of today's jobs?

1 rebellion [rɪ`bɛljən] (n.) 叛亂
2 execute [`ɛksɪ,kjut] (v.) 處死
3 maximize [`mæksə,maɪz] (v.) 使增加至最大限度
4 automation [,ɔtə`meʃən] (n.) 自動化

 B2 Preliminary English Test Reading Part 1

A group of friends are organizing a fancy-dress party on the theme of The Invisible Man. Read each text: What does it say? Tick (✓) the correct answer.

a

Send

> Jane, there's a rumor that five different people want to bring a white cat—is it true? It could be messy, especially if the cats don't get along. I think we should discourage the idea. Billy.

☐ 1 Five people are bringing a white cat.

☐ 2 Billy wants to tell people that bringing a cat is not a good idea.

☐ 3 Jane has a cat that doesn't get along with other cats.

b

> You won't believe this—I've found pink contact lenses! I already have the wig, the beard, and the white face cream, so my costume is ready! 👍 Paul

☐ 1 Paul wants to go as Marvel.

☐ 2 Paul wants to go as the landlord.

☐ 3 Paul wants to go as Griffin.

c

I think we should have a competition. Of all those that come as The Wrapped-Up Stranger, the one who keeps the full costume on the longest wins a prize (not yet decided). Amy

☐ ① The Wrapped-Up Stranger fancy dress will be the longest.

☐ ② The Wrapped-Up Stranger fancy dress will be uncomfortable.

☐ ③ Amy wants to decide on a prize.

d

● ● ●

→ | ✉ ⊘ | Send | ⚲

Girls, we don't all have to come as Mrs Hall, The Poor Woman From Downstairs or Kemp's Servant—we can dress up as a male character if we want! Sally

☐ ① Sally wants to go as a male character.

☐ ② The girls shouldn't go as female characters.

☐ ③ Girls should feel free to go as a female or as a male character.

e

ATTENTION! To all those planning to come as Marvel: We all know that he must be very smelly, but please be kind to the rest of us and omit that part of the costume! 😄 Jenny

- ☐ ① People going as Marvel should look dirty but not smell.
- ☐ ② Jenny hopes nobody will go as Marvel.
- ☐ ③ There is one part of Marvel's costume that people must not wear.

f

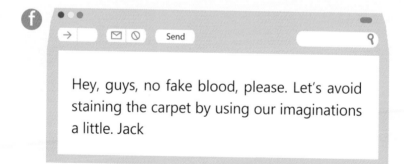

Hey, guys, no fake blood, please. Let's avoid staining the carpet by using our imaginations a little. Jack

- ☐ ① Jack's carpet is stained.
- ☐ ② Jack doesn't want the carpet to be stained.
- ☐ ③ Jack is bringing fake blood.

TEST

TEST

1 Listen and tick (✓) the correct picture.

a

b

c

d

121

The Invisible Man is the story of a brilliant scientist, Griffin, who is [a] _____ by light and discovers a [b] _____ for invisibility. After more than three years of [c] _____ he succeeds in making himself invisible. Griffin believes that invisibility will give him great power. [d] _____, he only knows how to make himself invisible, but not how to reverse the process. To his great surprise, he discovers that being invisible does not give him the [e] _____ he dreamt of and [f] _____ there are very few things it is useful for. As time goes by and his [g] _____ grows, he becomes more and more [h] _____ and violent. When he finds Dr Kemp, he has decided to start a "Reign of Terror" to get what he wants, and Dr Kemp informs the police. The police [i] _____ Griffin and find him but by that time he has already [j] _____ two people.

	1	2	3	4
a	astonished	fascinated	interested	attracted
b	invention	way	formula	method
c	experiences	exams	projects	experiments
d	However	Although	Unless	So
e	advantages	hopes	fame	career
f	that	which	then	too
g	emotion	horror	exhaustion	exasperation
h	jealous	invisible	aggressive	transparent
i	hunt	follow	search	see
j	destroyed	damaged	murdered	smashed

Project Work

Work in small groups. Make a poster or a video about a scientific experiment, real or fictional, that had a terrible result, and present it to the class. Find images and include answers to these questions:

a Is the experiment real or fictional?

b Where and when did this happen?

c Was the experiment carried out by one scientist or by a team?

d Who did the scientist(s) work for?

e What was the purpose of the experiment?

f Was the experiment successful?

g In what way were the results terrible?

h Was there anything positive about the experiment?

i Did innocent people die?

j Did any of the scientists regret doing their research?

k What happened to the scientists?

l Are there any similarities between this experiment and The Invisible Man?

作者簡介

P. 4

　　赫伯特‧喬治‧威爾斯（簡稱 H. G. 威爾斯）和法國作家朱爾‧凡爾納（Jules Verne, 1828–1905），被世人並列為科幻小說的始祖。1880年生於鄰近倫敦的布朗姆利，家庭環境一般。八歲不慎摔斷腿，臥床很長一段時間，父親便到當地的圖書館借書給他看，他從此養成求知若渴的閱讀習慣。

　　家庭的經濟狀況供不起威爾斯去上學，他便自己閱讀與學習。他才智淵博，學校聘請他擔任課輔教師。藉由教導年輕學子，讓他能夠支付自己的學費。他後來進入倫敦皇家理工學院攻讀生物學，畢業於倫敦大學的動物學系。

　　他的小說一出版就很暢銷，有些甚至被改編成電影。他創新的主題，成為科幻小說的經典。他曾經預言的科技躍進如今成真，譬如太空旅行等。月球背面的一個隕石坑還用他的名字來命名。他筆下的一些故事非常真實，奧森‧威爾斯（Orson Welles）曾經把他的小說《世界大戰》改編成廣播劇，讓大家還真的以為火星人入侵紐澤西。他的作品也涉及社會正義和人權等議題。

　　1946 年，H. G. 威爾斯於倫敦疑似心臟病發驟逝。

本書簡介

P. 6

　　現今許多人喜歡時光旅行、其他未知星球生物入侵地球等故事，但在 1895 年，也就是 H. G. 威爾斯出版第一部小說，講述未來之旅的《時光機器》時，當時的讀者僅知道兩種小說類型。其中一種類型是以過去或現在的真實世界為時空背景的寫實小說，另一種則是以各種不存在的世界、虛構生物和事件為主題的奇幻小說。H. G. 威爾斯（和朱爾·凡爾納）如同自己筆下的科學家，「發明」了嶄新的「科幻小説」類型。科幻小説是以未來的科學和科技發展為架構，《時光機器》一出版便造成轟動。

　　19 世紀末是科技大躍進的時期，蓬勃發展的科技新知突然改變了社會和大眾的生活方式，變遷速度飛快，也因此引發許多新的探討方向，例如：科技會對社會造成什麼影響？科學家是否走火入魔？最重要的是，假設某些事物在理論上可以藉由科技問世，那我們就應該主動創造它嗎？是否會有心術不正的人透過掌控新科技，來大飽一己之利？作家和讀者能透過科幻小說，來摸索自己對於科學躍進是否總是有益於人類和地球的想法。

　　1897 年出版的《隱形人》，是 H. G. 威爾斯的第二部科幻小說。故事以神祕陌生人於暴風雪中抵達英格蘭南部小村來開場，並探討科技發明面臨的一些難題。

真實世界 從驚悚到科幻：瑪莉·雪萊之科學怪人

P. 8–9

　　當科學凌駕自然法則之上，會有什麼後果呢？這就是《隱形人》的主軸。不過，這樣的題材在文學史上並非第一遭。瑪莉·雪萊於 1818 年首次出版的《科學怪人》，也是以這個為核心問題。

　　小說的主人翁維克多·弗蘭肯斯坦是一名出色的年輕科學家，他想讓屍塊拼湊成的人形起死回生。然而，這一個「生物」（在書中的名稱）卻形同怪物，弗蘭肯斯坦因而排斥他。這名科學怪人逃跑後，發現自己的外貌嚇人。他對維克多這位所謂的「父親」怒火中燒，便殺了他最年幼的弟弟。

　　科學怪人十分孤單，乞求維克多給他一個女伴。維克多拒絕後，科學怪人就殺了他的太太和好友。故事的結局，就是這場實驗讓科學怪人和科學家玉石俱焚。

P. 10–11

　　《科學怪人》提出了重要的探討面向，也就是科學和倫理道德之間的關係。這就是這一部享譽盛名的驚悚故事，何以成為科幻小說前身的原因。

　　之所以演變為悲劇，是因為維克多無法收拾自己實驗所帶來的可怕下場。他因為走火入魔的執念而進行實驗，卻未思考可能造成的後果。維克多試圖保護自己所愛之人，但是都沒有成功。他很清楚自己是造成他們死亡的真正元兇，因此背負巨大的罪惡感。

　　維克多無力處理實驗結果，讓自己所創的「生物」不得不變成怪物。科學怪人剛開始隱匿於樹林，並暗中幫助附近的一戶窮人家。他試著融入社會：聽著那戶窮人家的交談而學會說話；找到一些書籍後，開始自學閱讀和寫作。但是當他試著和那戶窮人家互動時，他們卻因恐懼而拒他於門外，這讓他感到絕望。

　　他很清楚，沒有維克多的幫助，自己永遠只能是邊緣人。他請求維克多給他一個伴侶，但維克多不願再創造他認為是罪孽的「生物」。他很怕如果再創一個怪物新娘，就會讓世界上多了一個邪惡的種族。維克多的拒絕，意味著科學怪人終其一生都要完全與世隔絕，因此他決定讓維克多也嚐嚐絕望和孤單的滋味。這樣的故事著實是個悲劇。

- 以人類智能創造怪物後，會有什麼後果？
- 誰才是真正的怪物？
- 當人類發現科學新大陸，對科學的應用卻駭人聽聞時，會衍生什麼情況？《科學怪人》和《隱形人》都能讓讀者對上述問題產生腦力激盪，至今兩部巨作仍廣泛地被討論著。

真實世界　你在看什麼？

P. 12–13

監控社會

　　自古相傳有一個人聽得到其他人在想什麼，但是這樣的讀心術卻常常使自己悶悶不樂。他感到很孤獨，因為他能夠這樣了解別人，別人卻無法這樣了解他。這一天，他遇到了另外一個會讀心術的人，彼此卻立即不對盤。

　　這反應出了一點，我們都希望有人能夠徹底了解自己，但我們也同樣都需要隱私。我們要能夠自由選擇了解我們的對象，以及該讓對方了解我們的哪些事情。即使對方全然不知我們的一切，我們也需要對方的信任。我們如果知道自己的言行受到監視，就會覺得不自在。我們需要一點「隱形」的感覺。這就是隱私權是基本人權的原因。

　　《世界人權宣言》第十二條指出，當隱私遭受干預或攻擊，人人均有權受到法律的保護，包括家庭、住宅、通信方面的隱私，也包含個人聲譽。

P. 14–15

現代人擁有多少隱私？

監視器

只要你走進商店、公共場所和許多私人大樓，穿梭城鎮或都市街道巷弄，監視器都會錄下你的身影。

社群媒體

如果你有社群媒體帳號，大概就能夠透過該平台來分享許多你個人的資料：照片、你所到之處、你的想法、和誰待在一起、正在做什麼、所轉發的他人文章、你追蹤的對象，以及你對任何事物的按「讚」或各種反應。

你的個人資料和所有活動，均被記錄下來賣給資料分析公司。他們會製作一份描述你特質的祕密檔案。你是如何設定隱私選項的？不認識的人也能看到你的網頁嗎？有誰能夠看見你的資料？他們又會如何運用你的資料？有誰可以讀取你的祕密檔案？你知道這樣的祕密檔案透露了什麼樣的你嗎？

手機

一想到自己的手機要是遺失了，你大概就會感到驚慌失措吧，因為手機顯露了你太多的「生活」。但你如果將所有生活大小事都儲存在手機裡，那麼隱私何來之有呢？你所到之處、每一封簡訊、每一通電話、你使用的每一種 APP、你所瀏覽的每一個網站，都被記錄下來。你清楚這些登錄檔會被如何處理嗎？你知道有誰能夠存取這些登錄檔嗎？

• 你可以接受哪些類型的監控？為什麼？
• 不能接受的監控類型又為何？為什麼？

故事內文

1. 陌生男子的到來

P. 25

二月二十九日，一名陌生男子來到易平村。他提著偌大的公事包，不畏冷風的暴風雪，從班伯赫斯特火車站步行而來。他從頭到腳包得密不透風，戴著藍色大護目鏡、圍巾和帽子，五官整個掩蓋住，只露出鼻頭。雪花佈滿肩膀和胸前，他行屍走肉般地踉蹌進入「馬車客棧」，然後放下公事包。

他喊道：「壁爐，麻煩給我一個房間和壁爐！」

他尾隨老闆娘霍爾太太走進訪客休息廳。她點燃壁爐後，便去廚房開始料理培根，再回休息廳準備餐桌。壁爐燃燒的溫度足以取暖，但這名陌生人未脫下任何衣物，她覺得很奇怪。

她說：「先生，我可以幫您拿走帽子和大衣嗎？我拿到廚房幫您烘乾好嗎？」

「不用了。」他看著窗外說著：「我想這樣就好了。」

「好的，先生。休息廳裡等一下就會暖和些了。」她說道。

P. 26

他沒回話。霍爾太太很快地擺放好餐具，然後走出休息廳。等她回到休息廳，男子依舊站在那裡。

她鏗鏘作響地放下煎蛋和培根，提高音量說：「先生，您的午餐來了。」

「謝謝。」他回答，仍一動也不動。

霍爾太太再度回到休息廳，她敲了門之後，未等回應就逕自入內。原本坐在桌邊的陌生男子，很快地起身，從地上撿起某個東西。

她注意到他的大衣和帽子都放在壁爐前方的椅子上，她盯著衣物說：「我現在可以幫您拿去烘乾了嗎？」

「帽子要留下來。」這名訪客回話時的聲音像是捂著嘴講話。

她轉過身，頓時驚訝得說不出話來。

男子仍戴著手套，拿著一塊白布遮掩住臉的下半部，所以聽起來像是搗著嘴講話，但這還不是讓霍爾太太震驚的主要原因。男子藍色護目鏡以上的頭部範圍，包括耳朵，整個都纏繞著白色緞帶，唯一可見的五官是粉色的鼻子。他仍繫著圍巾，粗厚的黑色髮絲從緞帶縫隙中竄出來。

她將帽子放回椅子後才張口：「先生不好意思，我剛剛不曉得您的情況……」

「謝啦。」他說道。

P. 27

「先生，我會幫您烘乾。」她說完就拿起大衣離開。

霍爾太太將大衣晾在廚房壁爐前，心想：「真可憐，大概是出了意外或是動了什麼手術，都毀容了。」

霍爾太太

• 霍爾太太為什麼認為陌生男子發生過意外？

當她收拾男子用畢午餐後的餐桌，男子表示行李箱寄放在班伯赫斯特火車站。

「可以請人幫我把行李送過來嗎？」他問道。

霍爾太太表示隔天可以派載貨馬車去領取行李。

「沒辦法再早一點嗎？」

霍爾太太找到機會探究這名訪客前來此地的原因，說道：「先生，因為路很陡，大約一年前，有輛載貨馬車在途中失控，造成兩人罹難。先生，意外總是發生在一瞬間，不是嗎？」

「沒錯。」

P. 28

「人們總是需要很長的時間療傷，不是嗎？我姊姊的兒子湯姆，工作時割傷手臂，緞帶裹了三個月。我姊姊得反覆幫他包紮和拆開緞帶。先生，希望您不介意我這麼問……」

他打斷她的話，「你可以幫我拿些火柴嗎？我的菸斗熄了。」

他的無禮惹怒了霍爾太太，她瞪著他好一會兒，之後才去拿火柴。

「謝謝。」說完，便轉身背對霍爾太太，望向窗外。

霍爾太太心想：「他對於意外和緞帶的話題很敏感。」但他的失禮之舉讓她惱火。

之後的一整天，男子一直待在休息廳。

陌生男子

• 這名陌生男子有何不尋常之處？
• 你覺得陌生男子為什麼無禮？
• 如果有人對你無禮，你會有何行動或口頭表示？請和夥伴討論。

2. 泰迪·亨佛瑞先生的第一印象

P. 29

四點一到，霍爾太太很想鼓起勇氣去休息廳，為陌生男子送上一些茶飲。這時，修理鐘錶的泰迪·亨佛瑞來到酒吧區，霍爾太太趁機請他檢查休息廳的老鐘。

她敲了門，走進去，發現客人正睡在扶手椅上，包著繃帶的頭斜倚著椅背。休息廳內唯一的光線來自壁爐，護目鏡因為反射而有亮光，臉部的其餘部分則是一片漆黑。她差點以為男子有著一張占據全臉下半部的血盆大口。這時男子醒來，趕緊用戴著手套的手掌搗住嘴。

她帶了燭燈走進去，男子的樣子看得清楚些。他仍抓著白布遮掩住臉部，所以霍爾太太看不到他的嘴。

她心想：「好吧，剛剛可能只是影子而已。」

她問道：「先生，您介意師傅來檢查一下時鐘嗎？」

他回答：「請進。」

P. 31

亨佛瑞先生走進來看見陌生男子時，立刻停下腳步。

陌生男子向他打招呼，然後詢問說：「你已經安排好去領取我放在班伯赫斯特火車站的行李了嗎？」

霍爾太太表示：「是的。郵差明天早上就會送過來。」

陌生男子說：「謝謝。稍早的時候，我實在又冷又疲憊，沒有力氣說明我是科學家。我的行李裡面裝有設備。我希望能夠單獨進行研究，因此請別打擾我。我出過意外，雙眼有時會很刺痛，要長時間待在昏暗處。所以，當我不舒服的時候，一丁點的打擾都會嚴重地干擾到我。這樣清楚了嗎？」

「先生，我知道了。」霍爾太太說完便離開休息廳。

亨佛瑞先生開始慢條斯理地檢查老鐘，想打探這名陌生男子的來歷。

亨佛瑞先生開口：「天氣……」

「你怎麼不快點結束檢查就離開呢？」陌生男子以惱怒的口氣說道：「這又不是什麼複雜的活兒。」

「好的，先生。」亨佛瑞先生趕緊結束檢查離去，但心裡很是不開心。

P. 32

他在村子裡遇見霍爾太太的丈夫時，和他聊起了陌生男子的事。

「看起來是一種偽裝，對不對？」亨佛瑞先生表示：「他住了下來，卻沒有告知大名。明天還會送來一堆行李。他說是設備，但誰知道呢？說不定是其他的東西。」

研究

- 陌生男子透露了哪些工作內容和自己的工作習慣？
- 你相信他說的話嗎？和夥伴分享想法。

3. 一千零一瓶

P. 33

隔天，郵差駕著載貨馬車，送來了陌生男子的行李。霍爾先生在客棧外頭等候，準備將行李帶進客棧，一邊和郵差的狗玩了起來。

男子照例從頭包到腳地走出來。郵差的狗一見到他，立刻狂吠。郵差還來不及制止，狗就已經咬了男子一口，扯破他的手套和褲管。陌生男子立刻衝回客棧樓上的房間裡。

霍爾先生說道：「我最好去看一下要不要緊。」

他上樓後，看見門沒關，就走了進去。

房間裡面很昏暗，他只看到一隻沒有手掌的手臂，接著就被粗暴地重擊胸膛，推出房外。門在他面前被甩上後便上鎖。

他一臉錯愕地站了一會兒，才走出客棧。

P. 34

過了一會兒，狗又開始狂吠。

「快一點！」陌生男子站在門邊，以暴怒的口氣大吼。他一樣全身包覆衣物，只是換上另一副手套和長褲。

「先生，您有沒有受傷？」郵差表示：「我真的很抱歉，狗牠……」

「我毫髮無傷。」男子回話：「把我的行李搬進來。」

行李送進休息廳後，陌生男子很快地拆箱。裡面放著上百個試管和瓶罐，裡面裝有各種顏色粉末和液體，有些還標示著「有毒」。拆箱完畢之後，男子便開始工作。

霍爾太太送上晚餐時，男子因為太專注，沒有注意到她進來，直到她將食物放在餐桌上。之後他轉頭看了一下，又很快轉開。她發現男子沒有戴護目鏡，眼窩的樣子異常的空洞。

空洞

- 這本小說的書名是什麼？
- 「隱形」的意思是什麼？
- 有哪些蛛絲馬跡讓我們認為陌生男子可能是個隱形人？
- 如果你是霍爾夫婦，你做何感想？

P. 35

他再次戴上護目鏡，然後轉身對霍爾太太說：「沒有敲門的話，請別進來。」他的口氣很不耐煩，這已經成了他現在慣有的語氣。

「我有敲門，但您……」

「或許你有敲門，但是我的研究──我這個十萬火急的必要研究──只要些微的干擾……所以我一定要請你遵守……」

他的舉止古怪，又具侵略性，霍爾太太害怕了起來，也感到不耐煩。

「好的，先生。您其實隨時都能上鎖。」

「我知道。」陌生男子說。他轉過身，背對霍爾太太坐下。

男子一整個下午都鎖在休息廳裡做研究。霍爾太太一度聽到了瓶瓶罐罐碰撞在一起的聲音，她跑去靠在門上偷聽裡面的情況。

「我沒辦法繼續下去。」他語無倫次地說著：「我已經無法承受了！這樣會賠上我的一輩子！蠢材！蠢材！」

然後一切又歸於寧靜。

4. 牧師家的竊盜事件

P. 37

這期間沒有什麼事情發生，直到聖靈降臨節那一天。陌生男子整天待在休息廳做研究，完全與世隔絕。他多數的時候都處在極度易怒的狀態，還會偶爾暴怒打破一、兩件物品，並且常常自言自語。霍爾太太雖然想仔細偷聽看看，但始終聽不懂來龍去脈。村裡的孩子給他起了各種綽號，大家都對他避而遠之。

聖靈降臨節那一天，牧師家裡遭竊。牧師娘邦廷太太在破曉前驚醒，她感到有異狀，好像有人入侵家裡。她聽到赤腳躡手躡腳的聲音後，盡可能小聲地叫醒丈夫。邦廷先生在黑暗中戴上眼鏡，走到樓梯口聽聽有何動靜。他聽見樓下書房有點吵雜，伴隨一個大大的噴嚏聲。

眼前最能做為防身武器的就是壁爐火鉗，他拿起後小心翼翼地輕聲下樓，邦廷太太尾隨在後。

P.38

屋內一片漆黑，靜悄悄的。之後有東西打破的聲音，還有翻書的紙張摩擦聲。他們聽到有人在罵髒話，並點燃火柴，整間書房充滿黃色燈火。

邦廷夫婦現在來到了走廊。雖然他們從沒關門的書房門口看進去，書桌抽屜是開的，燃燒的蠟燭矗立在桌上，但是卻看不到竊賊的蹤影。

他們再次聽到紙張摩擦聲——這次聲音來自牧師放在抽屜裡的積蓄。邦廷先生緊握火鉗衝入房內，邦廷太太緊跟在後。

「手舉起來！」他大吼，隨即震驚住口——因為書房裡面空無一人。

邦廷夫婦目瞪口呆地站在原地好一會兒，才開始四處張望。他們找不到任何人，可是積蓄卻不翼而飛了。

廚房裡又出現打噴嚏的聲響。當他們衝到廚房時，只看見後門開著，沒有人進出，門卻被用力地甩上。

竊盜事件

• 竊賊是誰？
• 你本身或認識的人遭竊過嗎？
• 遭竊的始末是怎麼回事？
  和夥伴分享。

5. 發狂的家具

P. 39

聖靈降臨節當天，霍爾夫婦一大早便起床。他下樓時，發現陌生男子的房門半開。之後到了樓下，才發現大門沒有鎖，但他清楚記得昨晚有上鎖。

他上樓敲了陌生男子的房門，然後推門入內。房裡空蕩蕩的，男子的衣物和緞帶散落在床上。他呼喚樓下的太太。

「他不在房裡，但是衣物都在。」他說：「他沒穿衣服做什麼去了？而且大門還沒鎖。」

這時，他們好像聽到大門打開又關上的聲音，還有人在樓梯上打噴嚏。霍爾先生以為是樓下的太太，而她又以為是樓上的丈夫。

霍爾太太來到男子的住房找丈夫時，目睹了驚人的一幕。男子的衣物動了起來，聚集後還跳到地板上，之後帽子直飛到霍爾太太的眼前。椅子升到半空中，四支椅腳朝著霍爾太太飛來。

P. 41

她大叫轉身。椅腳輕輕地紮實貼在她背上，迫使夫妻倆走出門外。房門用力被甩上並上鎖，一切頓時又寧靜了下來。

霍爾太太差點要昏倒在樓梯口。

「是鬼魂！」霍爾太太說：「別再讓他進來。我就知道他不是什麼好東西──他讓鬼魂附身在我的家具上！」

他們呼喚左鄰右舍，告知事情經過。不久後，樓下就聚集一小群人，開始討論對策。

突然間，樓上的陌生男子房門開啟。他們吃驚地抬頭看，從頭到腳包緊緊、戴著藍色護目鏡的男子瞪著他們。他緩緩下樓，之後走進休息廳，在他們面前甩上門。

發狂

• 「mad」有哪兩種不同的意思呢？
• 本章標題為何？
• 家具為什麼會發狂？

6. 陌生男子的盧山真面目

P. 42

陌生男子在休息廳待到中午才現身。大家聽到他常來回踱步,摔瓶罐和大吼。他憤怒的使用服務鈴三次,卻無人回應。

這時傳來牧師家遭竊的消息,大家開始拼湊推敲事情始末。霍爾先生則和一名鄰居前往警局。

這一天風和日麗,戶外的民眾忙著準備村裡的市集活動。而客棧裡,既惶恐又好奇的群眾聚集得越來越多。

陌生男子突然打開休息廳的門,瞪著酒吧區的人。

「霍爾太太!」他叫喚著。

霍爾太太手裡拿著放有一張帳單的小托盤過來。

「先生,您想看帳單嗎?」她說。

「為什麼你還沒準備我的餐點,也不回應服務鈴?」

「為什麼您還沒付款?」霍爾太太說道。

「我三天前就跟你說過,我在等一筆款項寄過來……」

P. 43

「我兩天前也跟您說過,我沒有要等任何款項的意思。您已經賒帳五天了。」

「我告訴過你,我還沒收到款項,

不過我手上有一些錢……」

「不知您的錢打哪兒來的。」霍爾太太說。

男子似乎被這句話激怒。他問:「你是什麼意思?」

「我的意思就是你怎麼有這筆錢。」霍爾太太說:「還有在我入帳或準備早餐之前,您要告訴我一些事。我想知道……」

男子突然舉起戴著手套的拳頭並跺腳。「住口!」他狂怒的吼叫聲,立刻讓霍爾太太安靜下來。

「你不了解。」他說道:「你不了解我是誰或我出了什麼問題,那我就讓你看個清楚。」

他鬆開拳頭,將手掌放在臉上後移開,他的臉部中央就像個黑洞。

「給你。」說完便給了霍爾太太一個東西。

她自然而然地接手，但當她仔細一看手中的東西，立刻驚聲尖叫，將那玩意兒丟在地上。原來那是陌生男子粉色又帶光澤的鼻子。

接下來，他開始拿下護目鏡，酒吧區的每個人都倒吸了一口氣。接著他又開始拿下帽子和拆開繃帶。

有人脫口而出：「喔，我的天啊！」

P. 45

預測一下

• 剛開始發生什麼事？用兩、三句話來說明。
• 你認為現在是什麼情況？預測看看後續的一些發展。再接下去閱讀本章後段內容，你的預測是對的嗎？

霍爾太太尖叫著衝向大門，每個人都奪門而出。他們以為自己會看到遍佈疤痕、毀容等明顯的可怕樣貌，結果卻是空無一物！大家跌跌撞撞成一堆，因為站在那裡大聲嚷嚷著讓人聽不懂的解釋的男子，竟然沒有頭。

街上的人湧入客棧，民眾立即聚集起來，對無頭男子開始議論紛紛。大家探頭探腦，想一窺男子的真面目。

霍爾先生和本村的警官傑法斯先生回到客棧。他們走進休息廳，看見一個無頭人仍戴著手套，一手拿著麵包，另一手拿著起司。

「你們要做什麼？」陌生男子說。

「先生，不管有沒有頭，我都要逮捕你。」傑法斯先生說道。

雙方激鬥了起來，陌生男子的手套因而掉落，這時有更多人加入了戰局。

P. 46

「住手！我投降！」陌生男子大吼。他呼吸沉重地站起來，沒有頭，也沒有手。「真相是，我人就在這兒——我還是有頭、有手、什麼都在，只是隱形而已。我知道很詭異，但隱形又不是犯罪，為什麼要逮捕我？」

「我不是因為隱形來逮捕你，而是因為竊盜罪。」傑法斯接著說。

陌生男子說：「我跟你回警局，但不能上手銬。」

「先生，很抱歉，這是規定……」傑法斯說。

男子突然坐下，鞋子、襪子和長褲都被脫掉。

「停下來！」傑法斯說道，恍然明白是這是怎麼一回事。他想抓住陌生男子的大衣，但一下子就撲空。

「抓住他！」傑法斯大叫，「如果他把襯衫也脫掉……」

襯衫袖子一拳揮往霍爾先生的臉

上，襯衫隨即飄落在地。

眾人紛紛喊著：「抓住他！」大家一邊互相拳打腳踢，一邊往大門方向和客棧外的階梯移動。

街上一名女子因為被不明物體推倒而大叫，狗因為被踹而哀嚎跑走。隱形人就這麼離開了易平村。

抓住他！

• 要如何抓住隱形人？和夥伴一起想想看對策，在課堂上分享。

7. 馬維爾先生

P. 47

湯瑪斯・馬維爾先生有張大餅臉、蒜頭鼻、闊嘴和造型怪異的鬍子。他身形龐大、四肢短小，戴著老舊的絲質帽子，大衣上用鞋帶取代鈕扣。

他坐在離易平村不遠的路邊，腳踩在水溝裡。一邊看著自己的舊靴子，一邊試穿另一雙，猶豫不決該選哪一雙。

這時，有點聲音說：「不過是靴子罷了。」

他想抬頭回應，卻驚見空無一人。他起身四處張望，仍不見任何人影。

「你在哪裡？這是怎麼回事？」他說。

「你別怕。」聲音回答說。

「你在哪裡？」馬維爾問：「你死了嗎？」

突然間有股力量抓住他的頸部並大力搖晃。

聲音說道：「很簡單，我是一個隱形人。」

「什麼？」馬維爾說。

P. 48

隱形人的手抓住他的手腕，他嚇得跳了起來。他的手指開始慢慢沿著隱形人的手掌往上觸碰，他發現可以摸到手臂，還有一張長滿鬍鬚的臉。

「太不可思議了！」他說：「你居然隱形——可是……」

他對著空氣近看了一下，問道：「你是不是剛吃過麵包和起司？」

「沒錯，我還沒完全消化。你聽好，我需要幫助。我很絕望，之後我看到你，心想：『你跟我一樣是邊緣人。』所以我要你幫我拿回衣物、幫我找到落腳處和一些東西。」

「喔，這我不知道。」馬維爾說道：「我覺得這一切都太離奇了。」

「我已經選上你。」有個聲音說：「你幫我的忙，我會好好報答你，隱形人很有力量。但你要是背叛我，沒有照我的話去做……」他停頓後，打了馬維爾的肩膀。

馬維爾被這樣的重擊嚇得叫出來，說道：「我不想背叛你。我會幫

140

你——只要告訴我該怎麼做就好。」

馬維爾

- 我們對馬維爾的生活有什麼了解？
- 隱形人要馬維爾做什麼事？和夥伴討論。

8. 馬維爾先生到訪易平村

P. 49

馬維爾抵達易平村時，村民正沉浸在聖靈降臨節市集的歡樂氣氛。雖然沒有人認識他，但有人注意到他。

賀斯特先生的店鋪位於「馬車客棧」對面，他看見馬維爾走進客棧後，沒幾分鐘後又出來。

馬維爾環顧四周，往院子大門的方向走去。他停在門邊，將菸斗填裝菸草，抽起菸來。他突然將菸斗收回口袋，走到院子裡。再次看到他身影時，他已經一手拿著裹住藍色桌布的大包袱，另一隻手抱著綁在一起的三本書。

「小偷，站住！」賀斯特大喊。

馬維爾開始逃跑，賀斯特緊追在後。但跑沒幾步路，就無緣無故地絆到，臉部摔到了地上。

為了釐清事件始末，我們得回顧

客棧裡發生什麼事。

P. 51

賀斯特先生剛看見馬維爾時，村醫庫斯先生和牧師邦廷先生都待在「馬車客棧」的訪客休息廳。他們當時在翻閱三本大部頭的書，書上寫滿各種難以理解的符號和數字，這時有人開了休息廳門。

一名陌生人走進問道：「這是酒吧區嗎？」

「不是。」兩位紳士異口同聲。

邦廷先生說：「酒吧在另一側。」

庫斯先生說道：「請關門。」

陌生人以截然不同的聲調回答：「好吧。」

接下來又以他剛進來時的聲調表示：「好，關門就關門！」然後關上了門。

兩位先生準備坐下研究這些書時，卻感到有人抓住他們的頸子。

「你們什麼時候學會解讀科學家的私人日記？」一個聲音說著，將兩人的頭壓撞在桌子上。

「我的衣物在哪裡？」兩人的頭再度往桌子撞擊。

聲音說道：「你們仔細聽好，如果不照我說的做，我可以輕輕鬆鬆殺了你們而逍遙法外。我要拿回衣物和這三本書。」

推理

- 和夥伴討論以下問題，並針對你的答案提出你的理由：你認為包袱裡裝有什麼？
- 陌生人是誰？
- 那個聲音為什麼需要那些書？

9. 大發雷霆的隱形人

P. 52

休息廳上正在上演這一幕時，也就是賀斯特先生目睹馬維爾在院子抽菸斗的時候，而霍爾先生和亨佛瑞先生則在客棧另一側的酒吧區。他們聽

見聲響、吼叫聲，接著寂靜無聲。

「不太對勁。」霍爾先生說道，一邊敲著休息廳門。

「你們還好嗎？」他問道。

對話聲瞬間靜止，又再次交談。霍爾太太前來，他們兩人告知剛剛聽到喧囂聲時，夾帶其他吵雜聲的情況。

「噓！」亨佛瑞先生說道：「那不是窗戶打開的聲音嗎？」

站在休息廳外的每個人都豎起耳朵聽著裡面的動靜，這時賀斯特先生跑到街上大喊：「小偷站住！」休息廳裡同時傳來聲響，接著是窗戶關上的聲音。

酒吧區的每個人都衝到街上。大家看到有人抱著包袱跑到轉角處，而賀斯特先生則臉著地的摔了個大跤。霍爾先生和兩位客人開始緊追小偷，但是不過幾碼的距離，霍爾先生慘叫，還拉著其中一位客人一起跌落在地，另一名客人一樣摔得慘不忍睹。

P. 53

越來越多村民跟著跑到轉角處。剛開始他們驚訝得止步，因為巷子裡空無一人，只看到三位男士跌坐在地上。等到他們又開始向前跑時，卻一一跌撞在彼此身上。

庫斯先生腰上圍著白色床單，走出客棧外說道：「阻止他！他拿了我的長褲！還有牧師的所有衣物！」吼

叫完後卻臉著地的跌在街上。

村子裡一片眾人狂奔、甩門的景象，沒過多久就變得空蕩蕩。大概有兩個鐘頭的時間，沒人敢走到街上。

這時，馬維爾正帶著三本書和大包袱，沿路走向班伯赫斯特火車站。

「如果你想再溜走，」聲音說道：「我就宰了你。」

脾氣

• 人們大發雷霆時會做出哪些舉動？

• 請看一下本章標題，隱形人為什麼暴怒？

• 你曾經大發脾氣嗎？和夥伴討論。

10. 亡命之徒

P. 54

傍晚時分，年輕高瘦的坎普博士坐書房裡進行著一些重要的科學研究，那裡可俯瞰博多克港的山丘。他往窗外一看，發現一名戴著陳舊帽子的矮小男人，從山丘上跑向山腳的城鎮。

坎普博士嗤之以鼻地心想：「又是一個相信報紙報導而到處高喊『隱形人來了！』的傻子。」

不過，在博多克港看見馬維爾臉上揮汗如雨又帶著驚恐神情的人們，卻不這麼想。他們駐足在路邊東張西望，一臉擔憂。突然間，彷彿沉重喘息聲的一道旋風呼嘯而過。

大家開始驚聲尖叫，從人行道跳起來，然後狂奔回家，把門甩上。

「隱形人來了！」人們喊道。

山腳下一家「歡樂板球手」酒館裡，酒館老闆、車夫、一個美國人和一名下班的警員正在聊天。

「外面在吵什麼啊？」車夫問道。

P. 55

有人步伐沉重的跑到酒館外，用力推開大門。狼狽不堪的馬維爾，哭嚎著衝了進來。

「他來了！」他用懼怕的口氣大叫：「隱形人要來了！救命！救命！」

「誰要來了？發生什麼事？」警員邊問邊上前鎖門。

「救我！」馬維爾腳步不穩，驚恐地哭喊著，但仍緊緊抱住書本，「把我鎖在哪裡都好。我逃跑了，他會殺了我！」

「你安全了，門關上了。」美國人說道：「到底是怎麼回事？」

大門突然因為重擊而晃動。

警員大喊：「有人嗎？是誰？」

酒館老闆讓馬維爾躲在吧台後方。有人從外面打破酒館窗戶，外頭充滿民眾的尖叫聲和逃竄景象。沒多久就全部安靜下來。

「我們把門鎖打開，」美國人說道，並給大家看他持有的一把小型手槍，「他進來，我就朝他的腳開槍。」

他解開門鎖，並後退了幾步。

「進來。」他說。

P. 56

馬維爾

• 截至目前為止，馬維爾遭遇了什麼事？兩人分成一組，一起把事件列出來。

緊閉的大門仍原封不動。

「其他門也上鎖了嗎？」馬維爾問。

「喔，糟了！」酒館老闆說：「後門沒鎖！」

他從吧檯衝去查看，很快又返回。

「後門被打開了！他現在可能就在酒館裡！」他說。

突然間，大家聽到可怕的吵雜聲和慘叫，馬維爾被拖進廚房。警員和車夫緊追在後，好不容易抓住隱形人，卻被拳打腳踢。幸好馬維爾脫身了，但廚房裡的其他男士，這才發現自己原來是在隔空打架。

「隱形人跑去哪裡了？」美國人大喊：「在外面嗎？」

「往這裡走。」警員說道，來到了酒館外面。

P. 57

這時空中飛來亂石。

「我來給他點顏色瞧瞧！」美國人大吼，並往亂石方向開了五槍。

一切寂靜無聲。

「拿燈火來。」警員說道：「我們來找找他的屍體。」

暴力相向

• 隱形人在本章出現哪些暴力的言行舉止？回想看看他曾有過的其他暴力語言和行為，然後回顧本書之前的章節來核對。

11. 坎普博士的訪客

P. 59

坎普博士聽到了槍聲。

一小時後，宅邸門鈴響起。家僕前去應門，但她卻未上樓回報是否有訪客，他便叫家僕過來。

「有人送信來嗎？」他問。

「少爺，是有人按門鈴後就跑走了。」她說道。

凌晨兩點，坎普博士停下手邊的工作，下樓回到臥房。他穿越走廊時發現地上有個黑點。他摸了摸，那像是乾掉的血跡。之後他往臥房走去，卻吃驚地停了下來，因為臥房的門把上有血。

進房後，他聽到房間裡有東西移動的聲音。突然間，帶血的繃帶懸空出現在他眼前，讓他瞠目結舌。繃帶似乎纏綁於某物體，卻又空無一物。他伸手去觸碰，摸到的是看不見的手指，他嚇得縮手，整臉慘白。

P. 60

他望著染滿血跡的床，床單也撕毀了。接著他覺得自己聽到了一個低沉的聲音說：「坎普！」但是坎普博士並不相信這種天外之音。

「冷靜，坎普，我需要幫助。」

坎普說：「不可能，這一定是什麼把戲的。」

隱形人抓住坎普的手臂，兩人大打出手，但隱形人更勝一籌，將坎普重摔在地。

「你如果敢大叫，我就打爛你的臉。」隱形人說道：「這不是魔術，我真的隱形了，而我需要你的幫助。坎普，能在這裡找到你真是太好了。我是大學學院的格里芬，你還記得我嗎？年紀比你小、高挑、臉色蒼白、有著紅色眼珠的那個白化症的醫學院學生？我已經將自己隱形了。」

「人怎麼可能隱形呢？」坎普說。

「很抱歉弄得到處都是血跡——血液凝結後，就不再隱形。只有活體組織能隱形。我又餓又冷，你可以借我睡袍嗎？」

坎普將自己的睡袍給了格里芬，又為他準備了點食物。之後他看著人形睡袍坐在椅子上，他盤問格里芬槍擊事件的始末，但格里芬累得簡直語無倫次。他講到馬維爾時，字句之間都停頓一會兒才繼續說下去。

P. 61

「那個流浪漢偷了我的書和錢。我看得出來他想逃跑……我真後悔沒殺了他！」

「你的錢從哪裡來？」坎普問道。

「我已經將近三天沒闔眼了。」隱形人說道：「很抱歉，我今晚沒辦法再聊下去。我得好好睡覺。千萬別透露我在這裡的行蹤，否則……」

「我不會講出去。你可以睡我的房

間。」

隱形人查看所有的門窗，確保必要的逃生路線。接著坎普聽見他打呵欠。

坎普

• 隱形人和坎普之間有何關係？

12. 先決條件

P. 62

坎普輾轉難眠，他去到書房，看到了當天的報紙。他翻閱易平村的所有版面內容，並沒有任何提及流浪漢的報導。

他心想：「他不只是能夠隱形，還是個失心瘋又兇殘的人！」

坎普到清晨仍未入眠，試著整理思緒來接受這一切難以置信的事實。他告知家僕，備妥兩份早餐送到書房後，就都要待在廚房裡。

早報送來後，他看到「歡樂板球手」酒館和名為馬維爾的男子的相關報導，但內容草率帶過，根本沒有提到什麼書本的事情。

他心想：「他是個充滿憤怒又危險的人……誰知道他會做出什麼事來！可他卻在這裡……我該如何是好？」

他到書桌寫了張短箋，並於信封署名「博多克港，葉迪上校收」的收信人，然後交給家僕去送信。

P. 63

格里芬一醒來就滿肚子氣。坎普聽見他在臥房摔東西，因此上前敲門。

「怎麼了？」他問道。

格里芬回話：「沒事。」

兩人隨即在書房吃早餐。

「在想出辦法之前，我要多了解一下你的隱形能力。」坎普說道，一邊看著食物從眼前這尊無頭又無手的人形睡袍上方消失。

格里芬說：「是這樣的，我離開倫敦後，就搬到切索斯托。我放棄醫學，轉而攻讀物理，主要研究光線。我深深著迷於光線。一個物體可以吸收光線、反射光線或折射光線，或是同時做到上述所有物理現象。如果物體不具反射、折射或吸收光線的能力，我們的肉眼就無法看見東西。」

「我知道，」坎普說道：「但我仍然不懂你是如何……」

「我發現一套隱形公式，讓物質可以像空氣一樣折射光線，如此一來，物質就會隱形。我都記錄在那個流浪漢偷走的書裡。」

坎普聽得目瞪口呆。

P. 64

「我發現可以漂白血液而維持正常機能的方法，我也能讓活體組織變透明，但卻無法隱形有色素的東西。然後我驚覺這項知識對我這樣一個白化症的人來說意義重大——那就是我可以隱形自己！但經過三年的實驗，我才發現無法完成這項研究。」

「為什麼完成不了？」

「我的經費不夠，」格里芬說道：「所以我搶了父親的錢，那筆錢本來就不是他的，結果他飲彈自盡。」

白化症

•找出出現「白化症」一詞的句子。何謂白化症？

•隱形人為什麼想讓自己隱形？

•他的初衷有改變你對他的看法嗎？和夥伴討論。

13. 大波特蘭街上的住處

P. 65

他們不發一語地坐著，之後格里芬繼續說下去。

「我搬到倫敦，在大波特蘭街上一家大型民宿租了一間寬敞的客房。我用父親的錢購買所需要的設備，打造我的儀器。我日以繼夜地進行研究，

就在父親輕生之際，我幾乎快完成研究了。那已經是去年十二月的事。我不得不參加葬禮，但我並不為他難過——我滿腦子都是研究的事。」

坎普靜靜地聆聽著。

「我的第一項實驗是將一些白色羊毛布料放進儀器，看著布料逐漸消失不見的景象，真的是世上最離奇的經驗。我自己都難以置信，伸手摸了一下，布料還在。然後我聽到身後有貓叫聲，原來窗外有隻白色的貓。」

「所以你將貓隱形了？」

「我讓牠隱形了。我先漂白牠的血液，用氯仿讓牠昏迷。然後將牠全身包紮繃帶，放入儀器。牠在即將進入隱形狀態的霧化過程中醒來，驚恐萬分的大叫。樓下的老太太上來敲門，因為那隻白貓是她唯一的寄託。我又對白貓加重氯仿劑量才應門。她問：『我好像聽到貓叫聲？』我很有禮貌的回答：『貓嗎？不在這裡。』然後請她離開。」

P. 66

感覺

•隱形人對誰沒有憐憫之心？為什麼沒有？

•你對本章的哪些人或事物感到惋惜？為什麼？

•你認為接下來的故事會如何發展？預測看看。

「整個實驗進行了多久？」坎普問道。

「三、四個小時。骨骼、肌腱和脂肪是最後隱形的部分，但是眼睛後面有顏色的部分無法隱形，所以牠醒來後，就像幽靈一樣──只剩兩隻眼睛飄來飄去。牠開始大聲喵嗚，當然根本抓不到牠，所以最後我打開窗戶讓牠出去外面。」

「繼續說下去。」坎普說。

「民宿老闆隔天來敲我的門。他說他知道我沒日沒夜在進行貓的活體實驗，他想看看我的儀器。他想知道我是不是在進行非法或危險勾當。我大發雷霆，將他推出門外後甩門上鎖，但問題來了。」

「大概到了中午，民宿老闆來敲門。我盡可能悄悄地分拆儀器，將組件零星放在房裡各個不同角落，以免別人組裝成功。他開門後，帶著兩個兒子和樓下的老太太走進來。他們看到房間空蕩蕩的，很是吃驚。他們把每個角落和床底下都檢查一番，但找不到什麼『可怕的證據』，他們感到很失望。等他們離開之後，我趕緊輕聲地將所有研究資料、寢具和椅子放在房間中央。用火柴點火後離開。」

P. 67

「怎麼說？」坎普問道。

「我的錢已經不夠我搬到其他地方，隱形是唯一的辦法。所以我把書和錢都放在郵局的寄物鎖櫃，然後讓自己隱形。」

「會痛嗎？」

「會。雖然是無法想像的劇痛，卻阻擋不了我。我看著自己的身體變得像玻璃一樣，骨骼、血管和動脈逐漸消失，肌腱最後才化為烏有。最後我筋疲力盡，整個早上都在呼呼大睡。得用布遮蓋臉部才能睡，因為光線會穿透我的眼皮。」

「接下來發生什麼事？」

P. 69

「你對那間民宿縱火！」坎普喊道。

「這是掩飾我的行蹤的唯一辦法。我無聲無息地走到大街上，開始盤算如何運用無所不能的隱形能力，而不用擔心會被抓。這種感覺真好，我就像處在一個盲人都市的正常人，但我很快就體悟到一些問題。我可以避開前方走來的人，卻避不了後方的人。所以人群對我而言，其實很危險。」

「對喔！如果大家看不到你，就會以為前方沒有東西……」

「完全正確，所以我開始走排水溝，我的腳因此受傷，因為排水溝比人行道還要顛簸，還常常需要閃避車水馬龍。還有，我是一絲不掛的，所以很冷，因為當時是一月，路面的污泥非常的冰冷。之後我發現狗嗅得到我的存在，狗要追著我跑、對我吠叫時，我就得趕緊逃跑。」

「這真是難以想像的處境！」

「我跑了一陣子後，才發現路上人潮過於擁擠。因為狗的緣故，我無法折返。於是我就跑到一戶人家的台階上，站在那裡等著，直到狗轉身跑走。」

「繼續說。」坎普說道。

P. 70

「然後兩個男孩在我附近駐足。其中一個人說：『你看到了嗎？』另一人問：『看到什麼？』『赤腳的腳印。』我低頭一看，發現他們正在端詳我留在白色台階上的腳印。男孩說：『有個赤腳的人走上台階卻沒下去，而且腳還在流血。』然後他指著

我的腳，我才意識到濺到腳上的污泥，顯露出了腳的形狀。他還說：『快看！好像是幽靈的腳！』然後他開始摸我的腳。」

「你有何反應？」

「我跺腳。男孩吃驚地往後跳，我趕緊跳到隔壁戶人家的台階，但另一個男孩窮追不捨，他開始大叫：『有腳！快看！有一雙腳在逃跑！』我死命地跑，直到雙腳暖和乾燥、不再留下腳印後才停下來。」

問題重重

• 隱形人隱形之後，遭遇了哪些問題？
• 你也想隱形嗎？和夥伴討論。

14. 杜利巷中的住宅

P. 71

「我又累又餓又冷，渾身疼痛，慘不忍睹，後來發現暴風雪即將來臨！我突然間閃過一個念頭。我去了應有盡有的『歐尼姆斯』大賣場，不只是食物，連畫作也買得到的那個地方。我在樓上找到一個安靜的落腳處躲起來，等到打烊。清潔工離開後，我就獨自一人待在偌大的賣場裡，拿了些

衣物穿上，還有一點錢和食物，然後去寢具區睡覺。」

「繼續說。」坎普說道。

「我突然驚醒，看到兩個店員走來。他們看到我之後，就開始追我。有好幾次我都沒被逮到，結果警察來了。我想到，唯有隱形才能逃脫這裡，便脫了衣服離開。我開始意識到問題的嚴重性，我無處可去，也沒有衣物可以蔽體，如果穿上衣服，就失去隱形的優勢。吃東西也是一個障礙，因為在食物完全消化之前，是可以看得到食物的。」

「真是想像不到的情況。」坎普說。

P. 73

「我也是，而且還有其他的危險。霜雪、雨水、霧氣和灰塵，都會讓我的身體輪廓現形——我也不打算長時間維持隱形的狀態，之後我想到販賣舞台劇服的店家。」

「好點子！」坎普說道。

「我在杜利巷找到一家昏暗的復古戲服道具店，樓上住家也很昏暗。店裡沒人，我就直接進去，但開門後才發現門鈴作響。所以我就讓大門開著，然後躲起來，等等看有沒有人出現。一個瘦弱、矮小、駝背、眉毛粗濃、手長卻腿短又彎曲的人，從後門走進來。他說：『又是那些臭小子！』他關上前門，又往後門走去。我想尾隨在後，但他聽到我的腳步聲後停了下來，然後他飛快地走向後門，在我面前甩門離去。」

「你為什麼想要去樓上的住家？」坎普問道。

「因為店裡面沒有我能用的東西，我想也許他家裡有更多的存貨。他又回來看一下店裡的情況，這時後門沒關，我就走了進去。結果那是一個小房間，但還有另一扇緊閉的門通往樓上的住家。所以我等他折返來打開這道門，然後在他上樓的時候緊跟在後。他突然停下腳步，似乎在聽有什麼動靜，我差點撞到他。」

「那個人的聽力真靈！」坎普說道。

P. 75

「沒錯。我剛開始跟不上他,他不斷地進出房間,在我面前甩門。住家非常老舊,到處都是老鼠。我終於設法進到一間戲服室,但他聽到我的聲音,手裡拿著小手槍走進來。他四處張望後,就走了出去,並把門鎖上。我聲東擊西讓他折返,等他進來後,我拿了張椅子打昏他。然後在他嘴裡塞塊布,把他綁起來。」

「他就這樣被五花大綁留在那裡?」

「這是不得已的。然後我搜查了整間屋子,找到了假鼻子、護目鏡、假髮、衣鞋等所需用品,還有一些錢。我照了一下鏡子,當然看起來很詭異,但還堪用,所以我走回街上,大家似乎不會特別注意我。」

「接下來怎麼了?」坎普問道,一邊望向窗子。

「好了,我領悟到,如果想在大庭廣眾下吃東西,就得顯露出這張隱形的臉。我仔細思考後,坎普,我體會到隱形人這個想法既愚蠢又瘋狂。我琢磨著,讓自己隱形就可以得到多數人想要擁有的東西——卻無法讓自己好好地享用這些東西。」

P. 76

「那你為什麼要去易平村?」坎普說,著急地希望格里芬繼續說下去。

「我去那裡做研究,想找到破解隱形能力的方法,我希望能夠在完成我的計畫後,就不再隱形。我現在就要切入正題和你討論。」

領悟

• 隱形人領悟到哪些重要的事物?

• 他提出哪些理由?

• 他現階段想做什麼?

• 你對他有何想法?請說明原因。

15. 無疾而終的計畫

P. 77

坎普望了一下窗外，看見有三個人正往宅邸過來。他站起身來，不想讓格里芬瞧見。

「所以，你現在有何計畫？」他問。

「我要從流浪漢那裡拿回我的書，你知道他人在哪裡嗎？」

「他在鎮上的警局，他是自己要求警局收留他的。」坎普語帶緊張地說著，聽到了外面傳來腳步聲。

「我錯就錯在於以為可以獨力完成。」格里芬說道：「我需要夥伴，還有能夠讓我睡覺、吃飯、休息的藏匿之處。」

「繼續說。」坎普說道，一邊仔細聽著屋外的任何動靜。

「我體悟到，只有在想逃離和接近他人的時候，隱形能力才有用武之地，因此特別有利於殺戮。我可以走到武裝的人身邊殺人逃逸，所以我們一定要以殺人為手段。」

「為什麼要殺人？」坎普問。

「只有透過恐怖統治的方式，我的隱形能力才占有優勢。隱形人必須讓人心生畏懼，控制博多克港等城鎮。所有人都要遵循隱形人的指令，違者格殺勿論，連黨羽也不放過。」

P. 79

恐懼

• 隱形人打算怎麼做？
• 他要如何讓民眾心生畏懼？
• 你有哪些恐懼？

坎普聽見前門打開又關上的聲音。

「但你會讓同夥陷入困境。」坎普說道。

「不會有人知道他的同夥身分。」格里芬說道，突然話鋒一轉：「噓！樓下怎麼了？」

「沒事。」坎普突然提高音量、語調急促地說：「我不同意，格里芬，你為什麼要用泯滅人性的方法？這樣怎麼能心安理得？別這麼做，你反而可以公開研究成果，還有……」

格里芬打斷他的話，低聲說道：「有人在樓下。」

「你在胡思亂想。」坎普說道。

P. 80

「我看一下。」格里芬說道，然後往門口走去。

說時遲那時快，坎普前去阻擋格里芬。格里芬先是愣了一下，然後大吼：「你這個叛徒！」睡袍突然褪去。

坎普趕緊跑出書房甩上門，他想上鎖，但鑰匙掉到地上。之後他用全身的力量盡量擋住門，但格里芬還是設法擠出了一道門縫。隱形的手指掐

住坎普的喉嚨，坎普為了自保而放開了門把。格里芬趁機撞門而出，坎普則摔倒在地。

坎普的收信人葉迪上校，是博多克港警局的局長。他正要上樓，看到坎普突然在和書房房門對抗卻倒落在地的景象。葉迪被看不見的莫名物體重擊，滾到了樓梯底。他聽到走廊上的兩名警官大吼追人。前門被重重的甩上。

坎普跟蹌下樓，模樣狼狽不堪，嘴角滲血。

「他不見了！我們只能聽天由命！」他大喊。

16. 追捕隱形人

P. 81

「他瘋了，」坎普說道：「而且做出不人道又非常自私自利的事，他只想到自己。已經有很多人因他受傷，而他即將大開殺戒，我們一定要阻止這一切。」

葉迪說道：「我們一定要抓住他，應該怎麼做？」

坎普說道：「你要派出所有手下，避免他離開這一區。監視每班火車、交通和貨運要道。他想從你警局扣留的某人身上，拿回他重視的一些筆記本。那個人叫馬維爾。」

「我知道這個人，」葉迪說道：「但這個流浪漢說書不在他身上。」

「他以為流浪漢霸占他的書。不管白天夜晚，一定要杜絕他覓食或睡覺的機會。每個人都要保持警戒狀態，只要有食物的地方全部上鎖。民眾一樣要緊鎖門窗。我們要在全區佈下天羅地網。還有善用警犬，狗能嗅聞到他的存在，他很怕狗。」

「很好。」葉迪說道：「還有其他要注意的事嗎？」

「他只要一吃東西，食物在未消化之前都清晰可見，所以他得躲起來進食。總之地毯式的搜索，還有藏匿所有武器。他沒辦法長時間隨身攜帶任何武器，否則會暴露行蹤。但他只要悄悄接近，就能設法隨手以任何物品殺了對方。」

「我會趕緊安排妥當。」葉迪說道。

P. 82

警方迅速地完成所有的部署。原本在兩點以前，隱形人還有可能逃得出這個區域，但兩點過後，已經難如登天。所有交通運輸工具都進入最高警戒狀態，博多克港方圓二十英里的範圍內，隨處可見三人或四人一組的警隊，他們帶著警槍、警棍和警犬，搜查所有的道路和田地。

警方

• 警方想怎麼做？

騎警巡邏郊外，挨家挨戶警示人民緊鎖門窗。所有學校暫時關閉，將學童送回家。不過當天傍晚，維克斯迪先生被殺的消息，使得全區的民眾都人心惶惶。

維克斯迪先生約莫四十五、六歲，看見他生前最後身影的人，是正在穿越田野的一個女孩。她說維克斯迪狀似想要搆著什麼東西，但她看不清楚。只有失心瘋的行為才能解釋這起凶殺案。隱形人用鐵棒攻擊一個不具威脅性的人。他打斷維克斯迪的手臂，還打爆他的頭。

17. 坎普宅邸的圍城之戰

P. 83

坎普隔天收到這封信：

今日是恐懼蔓延的第一天。博多克港已不再受英國女王的庇護，而是我的天下。今天是改朝換代的開始——也就是屬於隱形人的年代。我將殺雞儆猴——眼中釘就是坎普。子民們，不准援助他，否則死神也會找上你。今天就是坎普的忌日。

坎普叫家僕過來，告知大家檢查所有門窗是否上鎖，並且關上所有木製百葉遮簾。他從臥房的抽屜取出一把小手槍，放入口袋。他寫了張短箋，拿給家僕送交葉迪。

P. 84

「你不會有危險的。」他對家僕說。

他心想：「我們一定能逮到他！我就是誘餌。」

突然，他聽見前門的門鈴作響。原來是葉迪。

「隱形人攻擊了你的家僕！」他說：「他從家僕手中搶走你的短箋，他就在附近。短箋裡寫了什麼？」

坎普給葉迪看了隱形人的來信。

「我在短箋裡提議設下陷阱，」坎

普説道：「但我卻笨到讓家僕送短箋出去。」

樓上出現玻璃碎裂的聲響。

「是窗戶！」坎普大吼。碎裂聲接續此起彼落。

「他想從外面打破所有窗戶，」坎普説道：「但他太傻了，百葉遮簾都關上了，碎玻璃只會往外掉，割傷他的腳。」

「你有槍嗎？」葉迪説。

「有，但我只有一把，裡面裝有五顆子彈。」

「把槍給我。我現在去警局帶警犬過來。我會把槍還給你，」葉迪説道：「你在這裡很安全。」

坎普將手槍交給葉迪，並走向前門邊，盡可能無聲地解開門鎖。

葉迪很快地出去，快到花園大門時，卻聽見隱形人説道：「站住！」

葉迪停下腳步。

隱形人説：「你要去哪裡？」

P. 85

葉迪緩慢説出口：「我要去哪裡，是我的事。」

話還沒講完，他就被打到往後跌。他抽出手槍開槍，卻被奪走手裡的武器。

隱形人大笑。葉迪看見手槍懸空在他的頭上。

「起來，不要想耍任何把戲，回去屋子裡待著。」隱形人説道。

坎普待在書房，他蹲在碎玻璃之間，透過窗台邊緣窺看外面的動靜。

他看見葉迪在講話，心想：「他為什麼不開槍？」

之後手槍動了一下，坎普才驚覺原來槍在隱形人的手裡。

葉迪轉身走向宅邸，隱形人拿著槍尾隨在後。説時遲那時快，葉迪轉身想奪槍未果。之後他舉起雙手，接著臉朝地往前摔落，空中雖然瀰漫煙霧，坎普卻沒有聽見槍聲。

這時前門出現重擊的敲門聲。坎普以壁爐火鉗保護自己，並查看一樓的窗戶是否都上鎖了。一切安然無恙而安靜。

他回到書房，葉迪仍躺在花園。

但坎普看見家僕和兩位警員前來宅邸。

P. 86

突然間，屋內傳來重擊的木頭爆裂聲。坎普尋聲打開廚房門，剛好看到木製百葉遮簾碎片飛進廚房。

他心想：「他找到斧頭！」

接著，他看到手槍透過破裂的百葉遮簾對準他。他往後一躲，隱形人開了一槍，但沒射中。

坎普甩上廚房門並上鎖。格里芬又是咆哮又是大笑，然後再度舉起斧頭砍劈。

坎普心想：「他很快就會破門而入，這扇門擋不了多久。」

前門的門鈴再次響起，是他的家僕和兩名警員。坎普迅速讓他們入內，並再次鎖上門。

坎普說：「隱形人的手槍只剩兩顆子彈。他在廚房裡，沒多久就會破門而入。他找到一把斧頭，而且還殺了葉迪。」

葉迪

- 他為什麼離開宅邸？
- 他開了幾槍？
- 他發生什麼事？

P. 88

突然，他們聽見廚房門被劈開的聲音。

「跟我來。」坎普帶大家往飯廳方向走。

坎普進去拿出飯廳壁爐火鉗，交給一名警員，再將他手上的火鉗交給另一位警員。此時斧頭和手槍出現在他們跟前。

隱形人開槍，用掉了倒數第二顆子彈，並射穿一幅畫。一名警員以火鉗打落手槍到地板上。斧頭往他頭部砍下去，他應聲倒地，但幸好有頭盔保護。另一名警員則對準斧頭後方重擊，他似乎打斷某種柔軟的物體。隱形人痛苦地嚎叫，斧頭隨即掉落地上。警員趕緊踩住斧頭，再揮棒一次，然後手拿火鉗，站著觀察動靜。

他聽到飯廳的窗戶被打開和跑步聲。第一位警員坐起來，血從眼睛和耳朵之間流下來。

「他在哪裡？」

「不知道。我打到他，他可能還在這裡。」

他們突然聽見廚房地板出現赤腳走路的聲音。

「他從後門逃跑了！」第一位警員說道。

P. 89

　　他們進入飯廳。

　　「坎普博士……」其中一位警員開口隨即語塞。

　　飯廳的窗戶敞開著，而坎普博士失蹤了。

武器

- 隱形人使用什麼武器？
- 他如何拿到武器？
- 他用武器做了什麼事？

18. 繩之以法

P. 90

　　坎普往鎮上狂奔。路上空無一人，這段距離似乎永無止盡。他聽得見後方傳來的腳步聲，心裡惶恐不安。

　　一進到鎮上，他看見路邊有很多小石子堆。他路過「歡樂板球手」酒館門口，看到電車司機盯著他瞧，從小石子堆上方費力探頭看的馬路工人，臉上帶著吃驚表情。

　　「隱形人來了！」他對著工人喊叫，模糊地指著大後方。然後他轉進一條小街後再次轉彎，最後跑回大街，盡量引起眾人的注意。

　　他往街上一看，發現一名魁梧的馬路工人帶著鏟子跑過來，電車司機和其他人緊跟在後。男女民眾也從四面八方竄出，有些人還帶著棍棒。坎普氣喘吁吁地停了下來。

　　「他就在附近！」他大喊：「圍成一道封鎖線，從……」

想想看

- 接下來發生什麼事？和朋友分享看法。

157

P. 92

突然間，隱形人近距離重擊他。他設法站起來反擊卻失算，之後又被打倒在地。他可以感覺到肚子被膝蓋頂住。隱形人的兩隻手掐住他的喉嚨，但有一隻手的力道比較弱。

他抓住隱形人的手腕，聽到隱形人痛苦失聲。接著馬路工人的鏟子往下一揮，雖然看似空無一物，卻能聽到砰的一聲。坎普覺得有東西滴到他臉上，掐住他喉嚨的力量也突然鬆手。坎普使出渾身解數反撲到隱形人身上。他將看不見的手肘壓制在地上。

「我抓到了！」坎普大叫：「快來幫忙！我壓制他了！抓住他的腳！」

接下來是一陣拳打腳踢和呼吸沉重的聲音。

隱形人想反抗，但坎普沒有放開他。之後，隱形人突然尖聲哀號：「饒了我！饒了我！」還伴隨呼吸不順暢的聲音。

「後退，」坎普大喊道：「他受傷了，讓開！」大家開始後退，而滿臉瘀青、嘴角流血的坎普，似乎對著空氣在檢查隱形人的傷勢。

「他的嘴裡都是血。」他說道。

接著，「天啊！他沒有呼吸了，我感覺不到他的心跳！」

突然間，一位老太太尖叫指向某處。大家往她指的方向一瞧，竟看見一隻透明手掌的血管、動脈、骨骼、肌腱和輪廓正在成形。

「還有他的雙腳！」一名警員大喊。

P. 93

隱形人的手腳開始緩慢產生奇妙變化，並繼續蔓延全身。先是肌腱、骨骼、血管和動脈，最後出現肌肉和皮膚。隱形人的身體剛開始彷彿一團霧氣，接著瞬間恢復為完整的不透明人體。大家現在清楚可見他被猛烈搥打的胸膛和臉龐。

群眾開始退後，讓坎普能有起身的空間。年約三十歲、身上傷痕累累的一具年輕屍體，就這麼躺在地上。他因為白化症而擁有白髮和白鬍子，死不瞑目的眼珠如同紅色玻璃，神情悲憤抑鬱。

P. 94

有人開口：「蓋住他！看在老天的分上，快蓋住那張臉！」

有人拿床單過來包裹屍體，並將屍體搬入「歡樂板球手」酒館。史上罕見的傑出物理學家格里芬，就這麼結束了驚世駭俗的事業生涯。

坎普

• 想像一下，如果你是坎普，你會如何向朋友形容隱形人？和夥伴討論。

後記

P. 95

　　如果你想深入了解這件事蹟，一定要前往博多克港附近一家名為「隱形人」的小酒館。老闆體態臃腫，四肢短小，有顆蒜頭鼻。他會闡述隱形人死後，他所經歷的一切。地方法官想沒收從他身上找到的錢財，卻因為無法證明失主而只好放棄。

　　如果你不想聽他講故事了，只要問問他那三本書的下落就行。他承認曾保有那三本書，但隱形人後來拿走了。他說到這裡就會離開酒吧區。

　　小酒館每晚打烊後，老闆就會打開上鎖的櫥櫃和裡面的抽屜。然後拿出三本書，放在桌上仔細研讀。

　　他心想：「真是個天才！我要是讀懂了這些筆記，我一定不會重蹈他的覆轍。我會……怎麼說呢……」

　　接下來，他就會進入這輩子最甜美的夢鄉。

P. 97

酒館老闆

- 這名酒館老闆是誰？
- 那筆錢到底是誰的？
- 你覺得酒館老闆的夢境上演著什麼樣的故事？和夥伴討論。

盧德反抗運動

P. 114

「盧德主義者」一詞，現已泛指過於守舊而不願接納和使用創新科技產物的人。不過，這個名詞源自工業革命時期所產生的衝突，甚至延續至今。

盧德社會運動始於 1811 年的英國中部地區，據説是以搗毀紡織機的年輕工人奈德‧盧德（Ned Ludd）命名，但也有可能是虛構的。盧德主義者均為技術精湛的紡織工人，卻因為工業革命而失去養家活口的謀生工作。

P. 116

工業主義者和工廠老闆淘汰老練工人的原因，在於機器可由工資低廉的非技術工人操作，導致技術性工人失業，非技術性工人則在工資過低的情況下工時過長，工業主義者卻是越來越富裕的既得利益者。

盧德主義者籌畫抗議運動，經常砸毀機器。他們其實不是反對機器，而是希望擁有較好的待遇，讓技術性工人操作機器。此反抗聲浪越演越烈，支持者和日俱增，政府甚至派遣軍隊鎮壓暴動。 1813 年，於約克市進行審判的結果，共處決 17 人。

機器人的年代

從工業革命以來，企業家想讓利潤無限上綱的想法，促使新科技的誕生，以便加快生產速度和減少人力。

在已開發國家中，部分創新科技已滲透許多人的日常生活——我們很難想像沒有智慧型手機、平板電腦和家用電腦的生活會是什麼樣子。換句話説，整個社會已經透過消費能力來接納科技產物。

　　然而，數位革命仍帶來其他影響。隨著越來越多工作能由機器人代勞，負責操作機器的人員需求就會越來越少。而機器人能執行的工作，又無法以其他「人力」工作取而代之。換句話說，工作機會普遍減少許多。

　　而處於二十一世紀的我們，面臨的是另一個嶄新的自動化境界。無人駕駛車、機器人和宅配無人機逐漸取代運輸業和物流業的員工。現代的勞工會重演歷史，以抗議方式反對自動化嗎？還是新科技其實利大於弊呢？

> **Luddite** 盧德主義者
> [ˈlʌdaɪt] 名詞〔可數〕
> 反對新科技或新的
> 工作方式

- 請回顧你在第 113 頁第 5 練習題所寫的答案。有哪些主旨和盧德反抗運動有關？
- 有哪些主旨和現今工作自動化的趨勢有關？

Answer Key

Before Reading

Pages 18–19

1 [a] 2 [b] 4 [c] 7 [d] 3
[e] 1 [f] 6 [g] 5

2 [a] Mr Marvel
[b] Dr Kemp

3 possible answer

Iping and Port Burdock are in West Sussex, England. Iping is a real village. Port Burdock is not real but is possibly based on Southsea or Portsmouth.

4 [a] absorbs
[b] refracts
[c] reflects

Pages 20–21

5 [a] 7 [b] 2 [c] 1 [d] 6
[e] 4 [f] 3 [g] 5

Pictures:

shutters	axe	goggles
handcuffs	test tubes	a poker
a cart		

6 possible answers

[a] The people behind the Invisible Man couldn't see him so they didn't know he was there.

[b] People couldn't see him, but they could touch him and know he was there. Plus he could get crushed by a large crowd of people.

[c] People would be able to see him, or his outline.

Pages 22–23

8 [a] smashing
[b] exasperation
[c] punching
[d] startled
[e] aggressive
[f] gasp
[g] lose their temper
[h] stamp
[i] distressed
[j] raving
[k] irritable

Page 27

Mrs Hall

• Because he has a bandage wrapped around his head.

Page 28

The Stranger

1. He is unusual because his head is completely covered and he doesn't want to talk about it.

Page 32

Research

1. He is a scientist and does research. He likes to be alone and undisturbed when he works.

2. He has had an accident and sometimes needs to be in the dark for hours because his eyes hurt.

Page 34

Empty

1. The Invisible Man

2. It means impossible to see.

3. His eye sockets seemed empty. He seemed to have a handless arm and an enormous mouth that filled the lower half of his face.

Page 38

The Burglary

1. The Invisible Man.

Page 41

Go Mad

1. Mad can mean either crazy or very angry.

2. The furniture that went mad.

3. The chair rose in the air with its four legs pointed at Mrs Hall and flew towards her. The chair legs came gently but firmly against her back and forced her and Mr Hall out of the room. The door slammed violently and was locked.

Page 45

Predict

1. The stranger has taken off his clothes and bandages and now he is invisible.

Page 48

Marvel

1. He is probably homeless—an "outcast." He has old clothes.

2. The Invisible Man wants him to help him get clothes and shelter.

Page 53

Tempers

1. They punch things, become aggressive, rave or smash things.

2. He bangs the men's heads on the table, trips up/pushes/

hits people in the street, and threatens to kill Marvel.

Page 56

Marvel

- He agreed to help the Invisible Man.
- He helped the Invisible Man steal his books back.
- He ran away with the books.
- He was threatened by the Invisible Man.
- He ran away a second time to the town of Port Burdock.
- He hid behind the bar in the Jolly Cricketers pub.

Page 57

Violence

- **Chapter 10:**
  He hits the door, smashes a window, drags Marvel towards the kitchen, punches and kicks the policemen and cab driver, throws stones at them.
- **Other things he has done:**
  He punched Mr Hall in the chest, pushed Mr and Mrs Hall with a chair, slammed doors, smashed bottles and shouted, raised his fists and stamped his foot, fought

with Mr Jaffers, punched Mr Hall in the face, hit Marvel, banged the men's heads on the table, tripped up/pushed/kicked people in the street, and kicked a dog.

- **Other things he has said:**
  "I could kill you both and get away quite easily if you don't do what I ask." and "If you try to run away again, I will kill you."

Page 61

Kemp

They went to university together (at University College London).

Page 64

Albino

- "And then I realized what this knowledge meant for me, an albino—I could make myself invisible!"
  An albino is a person or animal without pigment in their skin, hair and eyes—they usually have white skin and hair and pink eyes.

Page 66

Feelings

1. His father and the old woman from downstairs because he is obsessed by his experiment.

Page 70

Problems

1. He can't avoid people behind him, crowds are dangerous, without clothes he is cold, dogs can smell him, and the outline of his feet can be seen in mud.

Page 76

Realization

1. That it was stupid and crazy to be invisible.

2. Invisibility made it easy to get things he wanted, but he could not enjoy them.

3. He wants to undo his invisibility.

Page 79

Terror

1. He wants to start a Reign of Terror.

2. When he is invisible, he can easily hurt and kill people.

Page 82

The Police

• They want to catch the Invisible Man by preventing him from eating, sleeping, getting weapons and leaving Port Burdock.

Page 86

Adye

1. To go to the police station and get dogs.

2. One shot.

3. He is shot by the Invisible Man.

Page 89

Weapons

1. A gun and an axe.

2. He takes the gun from Adye, and he finds the axe in Kemp's garden.

3. He uses the gun to shoot Adye and tries to shot Kemp and the policemen. He uses the axe to break the shutters and get into the house and to hit the policemen.

Page 96

The Landlord

1. Mr Thomas Marvel is the landlord.

2. The money belonged to the vicar and his wife—Mr & Mrs Bunting.

AFTER READING

2. COMPREHENSION

Pages 99

1 [a] F [b] F [c] F [d] T [e] T
[f] F [g] T [h] T [i] T [j] T

Pages 100–101

2

[a] Griffin makes his neighbor's white cat invisible.

[b] Griffin borrows Kemp's dressing gown when he tells him his story.

[c] One of the policemen injures Griffin with a poker.

[d] Kemp writes Adye a note suggesting to set a trap, but the note is stolen from his servant by Griffin.

3 snow, rain, fog, his strength, dogs, breathing, sneezing, dust, undigested food in his stomach, and his footprints

4

[a] By setting the story on the 29th of February he suggests something unusual may be going to happen.

3. CHARACTERS

Pages 102–103

1

[a] Kemp (or potentially Griffin).

[b] Mr Hall.

[c] Griffin's father.

[d] the boys.

[e] Mr Jaffers.

[f] The landlord's house in Great Portland St.

[g] Kemp.

[h] Mr Wicksteed.

[i] Mr Henfrey.

[j] An old woman.

[k] An old man who owns a theatrical costumes shop.

[l] Adye.

[m] Mr Cuss and Mr Bunting.

[n] The landlord of The Invisible Man pub: Mr Marvel.

2 possible answers

[a] Griffin and Kemp are both very clever. They are both scientists and do research.

[b] Griffin is violent and evil whereas Kemp is a good, brave man.

[c] Kemp and Adye are both very brave. Adye leaves Kemp's house although he knows it is dangerous. Kemp does the same thing and kills the Invisible Man. They are both rational and think about things before they act.

3 [a] T [b] F [c] F [d] F [e] T
[f] T [g] F [h] T [i] F [j] F

Pages 104–105

4 possible answers

[b] Mr Bunting goes down the stairs holding a poker.

[c] Mr Marvel studies Griffin's books secretly.

[d] The landlord in Great Portland Street doesn't trust Griffin and thinks he spends his nights vivisecting cats/experimenting on animals.

[g] The American shoots at the Invisible Man to protect Marvel.

[i] Kemp finds blood all over his bed.

[j] At first, Mrs Hall is worried the stranger may have had an accident.

4. VOCABULARY

1 [a] 2 [b] 6 [c] 7 [d] 1
[e] 2 [f] 3 [g] 4 [h] 5

2 [a] whispered

[b] muffled

[c] raved

[d] screamed

[e] howling

[f] exclaimed

[g] cried/shouted

[h] cried/shouted

3 [a] bandage, not a person

[b] tramp, person not an action

[c] injure, not a tool

[d] gagged, not a feeling

[e] shoot, not a natural reaction of the body

Pages 106–107

4 [a] gasp

[b] sneeze

[c] a bandage

[d] a spade

[e] yawn

[f] punch the stranger

[g] a traitor

5. Language

1 possible answers

[a] A white bandage covered all his head above his blue goggles.

[b] Somebody struck Mr Hall violently in the chest and threw him out of the room.

[c] Somebody slammed the door in Mr Hall's face and locked it.

[d] No one understood Griffin's books.

[e] Once or twice the stranger broke things with sudden violence.

[f] Somebody struck a match and yellow light filled the study.

[g] Somebody hit him hard under the ear.

[h] The Invisible Man took Marvel suddenly by the neck and shook him violently.

Pages 108–109

2 possible answers

[a] Mr Hall was punched in the face by the shirt-sleeve.

[b] Griffin was chased by two shop assistants around the store.

[c] Were the fields and roads searched all day?

[d] The door was suddenly shaken by a blow.

[e] Three men were tripped up by The Invisible Man and they fell on the ground.

[f] He was struck violently in the chest.

[g] How many people were attacked and killed by Griffin?

[h] Kemp's note to Colonel Adye was not delivered by the servant.

3

[a] sounds more likely to happen, possible, whereas
[b] is a total hypothesis and sounds less likely to happen.

[a] is the first conditional
[b] is the second conditional.

4

[a] If I found $500,000 under my bed, I would . . . [+ infinitive]

[b] If I eat too much tomorrow, I will . . . [+ infinitive]

[c] If my best friend rings me this evening, I will . . . [+ infinitive]

[d] If I woke up and found I was a monkey, I would . . . [+ infinitive]

[e] If there was a big fire in the building next door, I would . . . [+ infinitive]

[f] If I go to bed late at the weekend, I will . . . [+ infinitive]

5

(a) The only light in the room was from the **fire**, <u>which lit his goggles but left the rest of his face in darkness</u>.

(b) He had an enormous **mouth** <u>that filled the lower half of his face</u>.

(c) They heard the sound of rustling paper again—it was the **savings** <u>that the vicar kept in the drawer</u>.

(d) A stranger in a large **hat** <u>that hid his face walked in</u>.

(e) **The man** <u>who stood there shouting an incomprehensible explanation</u> had no head.

(f) "I'll show him," shouted the American, and shot five bullets in the **direction** <u>which the stones were coming from</u>.

(g) "It's all in the **books** <u>that the tramp has stolen</u>."

6. Plot and Theme

Pages 110–111

1

(a) 7   (b) 2   (c) 12   (d) 10

(e) 5   (f) 4   (g) 1   (h) 11

(i) 3   (j) 6   (k) 13   l) 8

m) 9

2

(a) 10   (b) 5   (c) 12   (d) 3

(e) 8   (f) 7   (g) 4   (h) 11

(i) 6   (j) 9   (k) 13   (l) 1

(m) 2

3

(a) No.

(b) No.

(c) Wells uses two narrative voices in the story. Initially the story is told in 3rd-person objective narrative, giving us the facts and the context. Then Griffin tells the back-story in 1st person narrative, so we can understand his feelings.

(d) This choice allows the reader to understand the reasons behind the Invisible Man's behavior rather than depicting him as a senseless monster. A similar technique was used by Mary Shelley in *Frankenstein*.

Pages 112–113

4

(a) Griffin's ability to make himself and other things (e.g. the cat) invisible.

(b) Yes everything else is human and real.

(c) Various answers possible.

(d) Yes, for the most part, he did.

EXAM

Pages 118–120

1

a) 2   b) 3   c) 2

d) 3   e) 1   f) 2

TEST

Pages 121–123

1 a) 2   b) 2   c) 2   d) 2

2 a) 2   b) 3   c) 4   d) 1

   e) 1   f) 1   g) 4   h) 3

   i) 1   j) 3

國家圖書館出版品預行編目資料

隱形人 / H. G. Wells 著；Donatella Velluti 改寫
；劉嘉珮 譯. 一初版. 一[臺北市]：寂天文化,
2019.9 面；公分. 中英對照;
譯自：The Invisible Man

ISBN　978-986-318-830-8 (平裝附光碟片)
　　　1. 英語　2. 讀本

805.18　　　　　　　　　　　　108012621

隱形人

原著 _ H. G. Wells

改寫 _ Donatella Velluti

插畫 _ Paolo Masiero

譯者 _ 劉嘉珮

校對 _ 陳慧莉

編輯 _ 安卡斯

製程管理 _ 洪巧玲

出版者 _ 寂天文化事業股份有限公司

電話 _ +886-2-2365-9739

傳真 _ +886-2-2365-9835

網址 _ www.icosmos.com.tw

讀者服務 _ onlineservice@icosmos.com.tw

出版日期 _ 2019年9月 初版一刷（250101）

郵撥帳號 _ 1998620-0 寂天文化事業股份有限公司

〔限臺灣銷售〕